Go Down Swinging for Love

The Boxers of Brook Street
Book 2

Sandra Sookoo

ARE YOU SIGNED UP FOR DRAGONBLADE'S BLOG?

You'll get the latest news and information on exclusive giveaways, exclusive excerpts, coming releases, sales, free books, cover reveals and more.

Check out our complete list of authors, too!

No spam, no junk. That's a promise!

Sign Up Here

www.dragonbladepublishing.com

Dearest Reader;

Thank you for your support of a small press. At Dragonblade Publishing, we strive to bring you the highest quality Historical Romance from some of the best authors in the business. Without your support, there is no 'us', so we sincerely hope you adore these stories and find some new favorite authors along the way.

Happy Reading!

CEO, Dragonblade Publishing

Additional Dragonblade books by Author Sandra Sookoo

The Boxers of Brook Street Series
With Love in Their Corner (Book 1)
Go Down Swinging for Love (Book 2)

The Hasting Sisters Series
The Devil's Game (Book 1)
A Second Summertime Courtship (Book 2)
An Impossible Match (Book 3)

Willful Winterbournes Series
Romancing Miss Quill (Book 1)
Pursuing Mr. Mattingly (Book 2)
Courting Lady Yeardly (Book 3)
Guarding the Widow Pellingham (Book 4)
Bedeviling Major Kenton (Book 5)
Charming Miss Standish (Book 6)
Teasing Miss Atherby (Novella)

The Storme Brother Series
The Soul of a Storme (Book 1)
The Heart of a Storme (Book 2)
The Look of a Storme (Book 3)
The Sting of a Storme (Book 4)
The Touch of a Storme (Book 5)
The Fury of a Storme (Book 6)
Much Ado About a Storme (Novella)
A Storme's First Noelle (Novella)
A Storme's Christmas Legacy (Novella)

Dedication

To Dawn Roberto:

Thanks for enjoying my books over the years and thank you for supporting the author community. It means so much.

Chapter One

July 30, 1817
The Albany
Piccadilly, Mayfair
London, England

A LEXANDER STAPLETON—VISCOUNT WEXLEY—SAT in his favorite leather wingback chair in his smallish drawing room, but the book in his hand simply couldn't keep his attention. The soft chime of the carriage-style clock on the mantel announced the ten o'clock hour.

Where the devil is Duncan?

He and his younger brother were scheduled to spend the evening at their club, but until Duncan arrived, there was nothing to do except wait. Granted, the man wasn't the promptest fellow, but he was now a half hour late, and there was no excuse for that since they both lived in the same building.

Closing the book with a snap, Alexander then put the volume on the rose-inlaid table at his elbow. His new residence had been cause for a bit of animosity between both his brothers, for Lewis, the oldest of the Stapleton boys as well as the Earl of Lethbridge, had recently married a month prior, which meant both Alexander and their mother needed to relocate. Obviously, living with a newlywed pair would prove awkward.

And truly, who wished to hear his brother involving himself

in carnal activities while trying to sleep in the room next door?

His mother moved to a townhouse in Hanover Square that Lewis had assisted her in buying, while Alexander went into rooms at The Albany, where many bachelors of the *beau monde* resided because they couldn't commit to a life of domesticity. It wasn't that he didn't wish to tumble into the parson's mousetrap just yet, he just wanted to build up a personal fortune for himself in order to attract a decent caliber of lady. One couldn't—and really shouldn't—pursue a woman with matrimony in mind if he couldn't take care of her, especially when he couldn't afford to purchase a townhouse of his own. Yet paying monthly for his rooms was a drain on his own bank account, for he refused to ask Lewis for additional coin. Which was why he really needed to enter more bare-knuckle boxing bouts.

And win them. Of course, that was the trick. Currently, his record of winning versus losing ran about even.

It was aggravating.

Besides, his nodcock of a brother went and got himself injured at his last bout which had ended with him proposing to his now wife, which meant he was no longer boxing for prize money, and that added strain to Alexander and Duncan, for their father didn't have much of a head for business—and he liked gambling a bit too much—leaving the Stapleton coffers near dun territory. For the time being, Lewis took on private clients who wished to learn how to box for whatever reason, and he watched over the salon like a brooding hawk.

Annoying habit, really. Why couldn't he go on a wedding trip and let Alexander and Duncan run the salon in his absence?

It was exhausting to worry about. However, he did keep the books for the Stapleton Boxing Salon, and with that came a meager living that allowed him to let his rooms, pay his small staff, and feed himself, but not much more. To say nothing of the fact that sometimes the numbers gave him problems and he didn't like how his brain felt during the struggle. The only break he had was when Cecilia—the new Countess of Lethbridge—

dropped by to lend a hand in balancing the ledgers.

Perhaps one day soon Lewis would allow her to take over that task, and that would give Alexander the freedom to find his own path.

"Why do you stare so hard into a cold fireplace with such a scowl?" Amusement threaded through Duncan's voice as he came into the room. "You are hardly the brooding type like Lewis."

"I can brood."

"You could, but on you, it's more pouting, since you're a bit slighter than him and not as attractive. And you're not an earl." Duncan snickered as he dropped into a matching leather chair. Though he was dressed in the same dark evening clothing as Alexander, his devil-may-care style made him more interesting and mysterious.

It must be the loosened cravat or the damned flirting.

"I am a viscount. That's enough."

"Only because it was a courtesy title of Papa's. Can't pass that down to a son."

While that was true, it only added to the heated annoyance already filling his chest. "As if you are not in the same position, Lord Frampton. Why were you late?" He tried to keep the irritation from his tone, but failed. The new circumstances and facing too much change in such a short span of time was quite jarring and he felt as if he were drowning.

"Don't come the crab with me just because you're living here now instead of in a grand townhouse." When Alexander made a crude gesture, Duncan chuckled. "My last lesson ran late, and I chatted with the man a bit afterward, then I had to tidy the salon before closing it for the evening. You know how Lewis is when we leave the salon messy for the next day."

"Yes, he's quite a prick about it, but I do understand that to a certain point. I admire your dedication to your clients." As well as to the family business, for Duncan had a knack for bringing in clients or investors because he was the most charming of them all. The man could sell fleas to a dog, truly. And now that Lewis had stepped back from public boxing lessons, Alex and Duncan had no choice but to divide those up between them.

Honestly, if Alexander had his druthers, he'd like to try his hand at being the salon's manager, for it was gaining visibility and traction, and the client roster grew each week. Whenever a boxer from their salon won an illegal match, it only brought interest to the salon. To his mind, he had a knack for overseeing several things at the same time, and he could use all of that to his advantage.

But Lewis was too damned stubborn to release that control.

"It's *my* admiration of coin that motivates me." His brother leaned back in the chair and then rested an ankle on a knee. "At least Lewis didn't cut you off."

He snorted. "Not that there was much coin to begin with." Shaking his head, he regarded his younger brother. "We are both making a living from the salon, though, so that's nothing to sneeze at."

"True, but my lifestyle is rather lusher than yours. I require more funding, and my creditors won't be content to wait forever."

"Because you are a bad steward with your coin, and a bit of a wastrel."

In that, Duncan took after their father, who had been a champion bare-knuckle fighter of some acclaim. So much so that he'd left that legacy to his three sons. Unfortunately, Alexander didn't have the same skill as his brothers. Where Lewis was determined and logical in the ring, Duncan was fast on his feet and more often than not took his bouts with a bit of underhanded verbal abuse and questionable movements. He, on the other hand, liked to feel out his opponents, and sometimes those delays cost him the matches. But truthfully, he just didn't understand the sport like his brothers, and his interest wasn't cemented in the ring. His strength lay in organization and overseeing the greater whole.

Which was why he hoped Lewis would let him manage the salon soon.

"Can I help if I'm more discerning in all areas of my life than you?" Duncan left his chair for the sideboard. "Brandy?"

"Yes, thank you."

Once his brother brought over a cut-crystal tumbler with a measure of brandy, Alexander took a sip as Duncan reclaimed his chair. "We are still for the club tonight, yes?"

"We are." Duncan nodded. "Should we call at home and ask Lewis to accompany us?"

Alexander pulled a face. "We could, but he's been quite pre-occupied of late with his wife. I'm afraid he'll be no company at all."

"It's so bizarre to think of Lewis as a married man." Duncan grinned. "I honestly thought he would hold out for much longer than he did before he jumped into the parson's mousetrap." He shrugged. "He was so adamant about remaining a bachelor even in the face of the responsibility to the title."

"True. I fully expected him to take a mistress for a few years, but you know how Mama is. She's like a dog with a bone when she wants us to do something." One of his eyebrows rose, and he took another sip of the amber liquor, wincing at the burn in his throat. "Damn, but what if she decides to badger me into falling into matrimony next?"

"Terrified of having a woman in your life, or frightened of being shackled to one for the rest of your life?" Amusement threaded through Duncan's voice.

"Yes?" They both shared a laugh. "I haven't had the chance to sort myself yet, don't know what I want for my life. Why should I ask a woman to stumble down that path with me and have her respect me while doing it?"

"There is that. Besides, a wife and then the subsequent children are expensive to keep. No sense going once more into dun territory just to have that." While he sipped his own brandy, Duncan watched him. "Do you want to know the truth?"

"Of course. There are no secrets between us."

His younger brother nodded. "I'm jealous, actually. Jealous of what Lewis has, you know?"

"What?"

"I am jealous of what Lewis has." Duncan shot back the remainder of his brandy, winced, and then set the glass on the table at his elbow.

Surprise went through Alexander's chest as he stared at his brother. "You want to be married? Have a wife, a home, a family?" He sat up straighter in his chair. "Would you give up the boxing to have a chance of that?"

"Oh, hell no." Though he laughed, it held an odd note to it. "I refuse to be tied down to any of that right now. However, I wouldn't mind having someone to warm my bed, as is what's happening to Lewis," he said with a cheeky grin. "The nodcock's canceled plans on me twice in the last week and I'll wager it's because he's using all that restless energy and anxiety to best advantage between the sheets with his new bride."

"Well, she *is* a looker." They shared another laughter. "But do stop. I don't want those imaginings in my head." It was enough to know that his brother had married. He didn't need anything else.

"There is that."

Yet if Alexander was honest with himself, and though he wouldn't admit to being jealous as well, he didn't want the hassle or the change in his life that being wed would demand. When he'd told Duncan he needed to sort himself before he could ever hope to attract a decent woman, that wasn't a lie.

"Lewis did have some luck when choosing Cecilia."

"Oh? How's that?"

"Well, the new Countess of Stapleton seems to enjoy boxing alongside him, or at least during sparring at the salon."

They came to the salon a few times together for such exercise, wherein Lewis indulged her by using the leather training mittens so she wouldn't be hurt or bruised. It was a way for

Lewis to continue being at the salon in a useful capacity since he'd retired from prize fighting during the last fight he'd entered. Despite conducting private boxing lessons if a client wanted them, his gimpy knee and shoulder prone to being dislocated prevented him from doing much else. In any event, it was entertaining and at times fulfilling to observe the two together; they were truly well matched, even in sparring, for the countess didn't back down often.

"So she does. What difference does that make?" Duncan wished to know with a frown.

"She has fit into his life apparently seamlessly. Even in the boxing realm, Cecilia enjoys indulging in that with Lewis. That is quite fortunate, don't you think?"

"Perhaps." Duncan narrowed his eyes. "Is that what you want, then? A woman who has an affinity for boxing?"

"It would help." Alexander heaved out a breath. "I don't think I could give it or the salon up, even for a woman."

Could he?

"Neither should you. Boxing is in your blood, and any woman who demands that you walk away from that life in any capacity is not the woman for you." With a frown, Duncan cast a glance at the sideboard, but he didn't leave his chair. Perhaps the effort wasn't worth it. "Wouldn't that be something, though, if we were to all marry women who enjoyed some part of the sport?"

"Except both you and I aren't looking for matrimony." It was Alexander's turn to glance with longing at the sideboard. "Let us hope Mama is too busy settling into her new role as dowager to remember that we are still bachelors." After having seen her bedeviling Lewis about his marital state, that was the last thing he wanted for his own life.

"You're right! She does have other interests now." Duncan's grin was wide. "Perhaps she will even start hinting around for grandchildren." He sounded almost giddy. "That leaves you and I clear to continue prowling about Town as we have before."

Alexander snorted. "As *you* have. I don't know I've ever seen you without a lady on your arm. Me, now, I can't remember the last time a lady looked my way with interest... Unless it's to ogle Lewis or you around me."

"Poppycock. You're not as ugly as you think."

"Do shut up." He tossed a house slipper that was on the floor nearby at his brother. "Ugly, indeed. I've got the best face of the three of you. Lewis favors Papa and you Mama, but I'm quite balanced."

"Yes, just like a mutt on the street." Duncan threw the slipper back, but the errant piece of footwear bounced off the arm of the chair. "Besides, your hair has this damned annoying bit of curl in it that won't allow it to be tamed. Ladies like that."

"Truly?" He'd never heard such a thing. "I thought they swooned for broad shoulders and tight arses or—"

"—large members?" Duncan supplied helpfully with an interruption and a cheeky grin.

"There is that." Another snort left his throat. Though he wasn't certain on how he fared in that arena compared to his brothers, for he knew his shoulders and arse had earned him more than a few covetous glances. One thing about boxing was it kept a man fit.

"Come. I want my dinner and there is supposed to be a French-style cabaret at the club tonight." He stood up from his chair and then drew a pair of white gloves from a hidden pocket in one of the tails of his jacket. "In any event, if Mama is distracted, I'll wager it won't last long. She won't rest until all of us Stapleton brothers are married, and not even happily. Hell, she was ready to sell Lewis off lock, stock, and barrel to the highest bidder."

"Yeah, how he managed to weasel his way out of her clutches is still a mystery." As Duncan pulled on his gloves, Alexander gained his own feet. "Of course, he was clandestinely stealing kisses from Cecilia well before we discovered his intent."

"How does one man who is so clueless about flirting or romance just happen upon a woman who has so much in common with him?" Truly, he had no idea. "Must be the damned title."

"Well, most women desire an elevation in society," Duncan said as he moved into the smaller room Alexander used as a parlor.

"True." Was that out of a need for security regarding the future or for the mere society position she could lord over her friends and acquaintances? "It shouldn't be like that, but I do understand." Damn, but he was glad he was born male, for his lot was better merely due to gender, and that didn't seem quite fair. "Say, have you ever given thought into the absolutely abysmal futures women are handed if they're not fortunate enough to marry out of a first Season? Not much to fill one's time, hmm?"

Why his thoughts had moved to such a topic, he had no idea, but ever since his father died and left his mother alone, he'd been pondering her fate.

"I have not." His brother glanced at him with questions in his eyes. "Why are you?"

"No idea." Alexander picked up his own pair of gloves, then donned them. "Perhaps it's because life is changing around us with Lewis married and Mama having moved houses, and me here now, as well." He shrugged and grabbed his top hat. "I suppose I'm just glad I don't need to wait around for some fellow to come calling or for my parents or oldest brother to arrange a match for me."

Duncan chuckled. "Don't worry. I'm sure Mama will turn her attention to you soon enough, and once you're matched, she'll practically demand grandchildren." He gave Alexander's shoulder a mock punch. "Hell, I wouldn't put it past her to pit you against Lewis in who can impregnate their woman first."

"Ugh. Don't put that into my mind. Nor do I want you to rush my fences." He set his hat upon his hair. "I am perfectly content in bachelorhood."

Mostly.

"To misquote the Bard, methinks you doth protest a bit too

much, though I suspect you will be a terrible husband," Duncan said with a smirk as he opened the door.

"How do you figure?"

"You're not dedicated, and you haven't been to any cause, even boxing." His brother shrugged as if it were obvious. "You only do things by half, especially when your heart isn't in it, as evidenced in your win-to-loss rate in the ring."

"Well, we all can't be whores for attention like you," Alexander shot off though annoyance rose in his chest in a hot wave as they followed the corridor toward the main staircase. "If that was ever taken away from you, I don't know how you'd survive."

"Speaking out of turn, brother. Don't blame me because you don't enjoy being the center of attention. If you would learn how to feed off the energy of the crowd, you might do better during your bouts." Duncan shrugged. "And a bit of charm never hurts either. In fact, business dealings practically depend upon it."

"I'll bear that in mind." Of course, he couldn't fault his brother for what he was good at, but knowing that he was rankled. It only made him feel his inadequacies all that much more. By the time they arrived at the curb outside the building, their carriage was in sight down the street. "Do you think Lewis will join us?"

"Who can say?" Duncan raised a hand to hail the driver. "One would think Lewis would take a few weeks' holiday leave from the salon and other things for a honeymoon of sorts, but he is quite stubborn and a touch controlling."

"Indeed." Relief slipped down Alexander's spine as the carriage came to a halt in front of them. "If Lewis does end up taking a honeymoon, or God forbid a wedding trip, you and I need to figure out how to manage the salon and everything that goes with that, along with teaching his clients."

"Then let us hope his stubbornness keeps him going. I would rather not have my days full of toiling."

Once Duncan climbed into the carriage, Alexander followed. "Agreed." Yet the feeling that he might be good at managing the boxing salon wouldn't fade. How to broach the subject with

Lewis and ask him to stand down without invoking his wrath? It might be a tall order, but then, at least he wasn't the earl and wasn't weighed down with other responsibilities.

Thank goodness for being only the heir.

Chapter Two

August 2, 1817
No. 16
Grosvenor Square, Mayfair
London, England

MISS LYDIA TETFORD sat in the drawing room of her father's townhouse with a cup of tea in hand and a faint smile curving her lips, for her father was telling her of the evening when he'd been invited to a duke's home. He'd thought it strange at the time, even if he was a gentleman and quite popular within the *ton*, but when the duke invited the assembled company into the parlor, there was a corpse laid out on a table, and he wanted her father to perform a postmortem examination for their amusement.

"Did you do it?"

"Of course I did!" His deep chuckle tugged a grin from her again. "How often is a physician afforded that privilege? But it rankled that I was doing it to entertain bored peers."

"Your integrity is one of the things I adore about you, Papa." She took a sip of tea. "Everyone should strive to be like you."

"I don't know about that, but it is enough that you and Ian are."

Ian was her senior by two years, and at eight and twenty, he had managed to set himself up as a physician at a clinic in London who worked mostly with wounded and maimed soldiers who'd returned home from the war and were forgotten by the government and now were shunned largely by society.

While she was exceedingly proud of her brother, it always brought around frustration on her part, for though Ian had gone to school and then was able to study at the University of Edinburgh for his medical education, she had been denied entrance as a student merely due to her sex. No number of objections on her part or inquiries on her father's—he was a professor there of some esteem most of the time—would change the minds of the powers-that-be, who were all old, white-haired men and thought themselves apparently God's gift to mankind.

And while Ian rented rooms for himself, she was stuck living at home with her father until that apparently "magical" day when a man decided she was worthy enough to marry. Such gammon.

"I'm glad you think so, for sometimes I think I take after Mama." Especially with her flame red hair and cornflower blue eyes and the spattering of freckles over her pale skin that bedeviled her every time she needed to go out into society.

"I would be happy to try and dissuade you, but you have her temper, so there's no going back." Her father snickered when she bristled, but when she laughed, he did too. "That is in no way a detriment. Your mother's temper was what first brought us together."

"That meeting is one of my favorite stories." And she'd heard it time out of hand, for her father loved to tell it during gatherings with friends. It was one of those tales that needed no embellishment.

"It was the truth, and I loved her to the last." Some of the gaiety faded from his face, for they had both lost her three years before, shortly after Lydia had the unfortunate luck to accept the hand of a large, lout Scottish blacksmith who often entered illegal boxing bouts on the weekends for extra coin.

Mostly to appease her mother. But then, she'd been naïve at the age of three and twenty, and it was her mother's wish to see her wed. However, that had been quite the mistake, as time had shown.

Not that it mattered now. Her mother had died from complications of pneumonia. The engagement had been broken a year ago. Lydia had completed all the coursework her father had set before her and had "passed" the exams that she would have had to take, had she been granted entry into the University of Edinburgh for medical education. What was more, she'd come away with higher marks than what Ian had scored when he'd taken the exams.

Yet by society's rules, she would never carry the moniker of doctor, nor would she be allowed to overtly and openly practice medicine.

It made her want to kick things or utter profanities.

"You have gone unexpectedly glum, poppet. Are you remembering your mother?"

With a sigh, she pushed away the bitterness and shook her head. "Perhaps, but mostly the fact I'll never be a doctor."

"Not by title, but you have the skills and the affinity for helping people. That makes you a doctor, and I would be delighted to have you in my clinic, especially since my time in the autumn will be taken up by lecturing at Cambridge."

Which was the reason they'd rented a townhouse in Mayfair to begin with, and it was a good change of pace from living in Edinburgh.

"I appreciate that." Though she often helped in her father's clinic no matter where it was, that didn't lessen the sting of never succeeding on her own merits.

"What else, though? There are shadows in your eyes, poppet." He set his teacup into its saucer and then put them both on the low table in front of him.

She did the same with her cup and saucer before meeting her father's gaze. "I'll admit that I'm frightened."

"Why?" Surprise jumped into his expression. "I had no idea there was anything wrong."

"I didn't want to worry you, but it's Colin."

"Your former fiancé Colin?"

"Yes." She nodded. "He won't leave me alone." She'd broken the engagement due to his refusal to support her dreams of being a doctor and practicing medicine. Even though her father had never demanded back the dowry he'd already paid to Colin, her former fiancé still managed to bedevil her, no doubt because his ego couldn't take the rejection.

"Is he threatening you? Even after we moved to London?" Incredulity rang in his voice.

"Not overtly, just in a few letters, but he says he's coming to London for some boxing matches. Of course, I think the whole thing is childish and stupidly risky, so I don't care about that, but I am concerned that he'll try to perhaps harm me or worse, attempt to take me back to Scotland with him." Shivery fear went down her spine. "What should I do?"

Concern creased his brow. "Perhaps you should learn how to defend yourself, since I know you're far too stubborn to stay in the townhouse where it's safe."

"Safe? From a man like Colin? Doesn't matter if his parents were respectable in Scottish society or if he can trace his family back to the clans. He is a bounder and uses that to intimidate others." Lydia slowly shook her head. "Perhaps I should carry a scalpel with me wherever I go."

"And slice your way through the *ton*?" He blew out a breath. "Please don't. The gossip alone will bury you as well as me."

There was that. "Then I shall fall back on what I know best, since I *did* learn the rudimentary basics of Japanese old-style jujitsu." At least the exercise kept her body nimble and mind calm.

"Ha." Her father grinned. "There are times when I regret your unconventional upbringing while I traveled through England and the Continent with your mother and you children."

"Why? It allowed me an education that was vastly superior to anything I could have had with tutors or in a finishing school."

When she offered him a grin, they both laughed. "Seeing the world, interacting with the people therein is much better than sitting in a classroom or going to a boarding school to be 'finished'." She shrugged. "What does that mean anyway?"

"I never understood that myself, for a person's education and growth—regardless of sex—is never finished."

"Exactly." With a wink, she took a honey cake from the tea tray. "Besides, my education was wonderful. I adored every moment. It provided lovely opportunities for me and Ian. I miss Kenji though." He'd been with her father's staff for a few years, traveling with them, and at that time, the older man had taught her and Ian how to fight like they'd done in feudal Japan. It was quite effective and oddly helped to calm her racing thoughts when she'd railed against the world because the stuffy old men in charge of medical training in Scotland refused to admit a woman into their hallowed halls.

We don't need gatekeepers for education or society. We need determined people who want to change the world. Make it better for everyone.

"I'm glad." He gazed at her with fondness. "You mother wished for you to be a grand lady, so she could have a laugh that a half-Scottish woman made it into the English *beau monde*. Of course, she'd always hoped Ian would marry a society lady, but he's more deeply entrenched into being a doctor than I am."

How could she forget? "I would like to be that preoccupied in my field of choice too." Yet that was still a fight, and probably would be for decades to come. "Thankfully Mama died before I managed to disappoint her." She frowned as her chest tightened with a pain she was well versed in. "I'm not one for embroidery, painting, or pressing flowers. I'm rubbish at piano playing and singing isn't my forte, but I'd rather eat a spider than sit around, wringing my hands and waiting for some man to take notice of me, to have him declare me 'good enough' for him to wed and have me bear his children."

No, thank you.

"Ah, Lydia, you were always a strong spirit. So much like

your mother." Her father's grin softened around the edges. "Thank goodness for that. I'd rather have a daughter who is willing to advance society by helping instead of spending time with frivolous hobbies that have no value."

"I appreciate that, but some days, it seems an overwhelming task in which I talk into a void where no one wants to hear what I have to say."

"It will get better, but you must be patient."

She snorted. "That isn't my strong suit."

"I think we all know that." Her father laughed, and that deep booming sound soothed her jagged edges. "Your time will come."

"Perhaps. Would that you can speak sense into the men with the votes who keep anyone oppressed who isn't like them. It is madness women are not allowed into medical school." Or do other things such as own property, but that was how the world was. Did she have the strength to keep fighting and essentially banging her head against the wall where her words fell on deaf ears? That remained to be seen.

"Change is sometimes slow, but mark my words, poppet. There *will* be change. Perhaps not in my lifetime but in yours. I welcome that day when women can work alongside men in professions where that unique insight will be useful."

"We can only hope. The female mind is not small or delicate, and I am growing tired of being told so over and over." If given half a chance, women could put forth answers and ideas that would enhance and change practically everything, but for some reason, the powers-that-be wished to quell them beneath thumbs and blustering orders.

Go ahead and fear us, you bastards. Many of our mothers were considered witches.

And that meant women wielded power, which they couldn't cope with.

"I can imagine, but you must wait. Your time will come when you can use your skills and talents. After that, you will be unstoppable, and the world will be better for you and all the others like you."

"Not soon enough." A long-suffering sigh escaped her throat. "I've the same medical training and knowledge as the men, yet my sex prevents me from acting upon it, and as much as I loved Mama, I am more than just a healer with herbs. Effective though they can sometimes be."

"I am well aware of that." He appeared as if he were wrestling with a problem. "Barring that, and in the interim of waiting, you can allow one of the men I keep inviting to dinner to court you."

Not you too, Papa. "Oh, not this again."

It wasn't that she was opposed to marriage—much—it was that she didn't wish to enter into that state right now. And the thought of bearing and rearing children almost made her want to run screaming from the room. Her life was fulfilled as it was now with the work at the clinic and her patients. Having domestic duties placed upon her shoulders would get in the way of that… or demand she quit altogether, and she'd worked too hard to gain even the tiny foothold she had. Absolutely, she wasn't willing to give it up merely to do what society expected of a woman.

"Hear me out." Her father raised a hand, palm outward. "I want to make certain you are taken care of once I can no longer do that."

Some of her ire faded. "I shall be fine. Aren't I always?"

"Yes, but unfortunately, we both know what society is. You need a man in some capacity, if only to help you meet your dreams. Take you further than I have been able to."

It was so dratted maddening. She huffed. "Would that it wasn't so."

"As do I. If worse comes to worst, you can work with Ian." For long moments, her father rested his sad gaze on her. "Since I've already given up your dowry…" He shook his head. "I can provide another, of course, because you *are* worth that, but I would rather not advertise such a thing, since your last engagement ended in disaster, and I want the next man you choose to want you instead of the coin."

"Thank you." It was all so... ridiculous. "I won't change my mind, Papa. You know this."

"Oh, I am well aware of how stubborn you are. After all, you have your mother's spirit and her hair, but if said man happens to tug at your heartstrings in the process?"

Love. That was always the fly in the ointment, wasn't it? Once love came 'round, everything would change, or perhaps nothing would, it depended upon the man. Perhaps. "I don't know. Romance is a distraction to all that I want to accomplish in my life."

"While I understand that, consider that it can prove a help instead of a hinderance. I once thought as you did, but then I met your mother, and I went tip over tail and forgot which way was up for a bit."

Her parents' romance was something she did wish to aspire to, but perhaps not just now. "You were happy though. That isn't the guarantee, and I wouldn't have had that with Colin." Thus just one reason for the breaking of the engagement.

"Of course we were. Your mother helped me to see that life isn't an all or nothing proposition. Once you find the right fit, it is much like magic, and not even medical science can explain it."

It made sense, and yet it didn't. Lydia sighed. "Still, I'd rather not chance it."

"Ah, poppet, please keep an open mind. Not all men were put on his earth to distract you or set you back or keep you under their thumb."

"I can take care of myself," she reiterated but she might welcome a distraction if it wasn't permanent. Romance was one thing, and something she wanted to avoid, but a fleeting tryst that could help to refresh her mind? Perhaps she might entertain that. The one secret she'd never told her father about was the fact she wasn't an innocent any longer. She'd attained the age of six and twenty without falling pregnant by the few indiscretions she'd indulged in, but then, she had taken precautions, and was a sight more intelligent than the usual naïve debutante.

Everyone had physical needs of the body, and to her way of thinking, there was no shame in having those needs met, even if society deemed them as shocking or scandalous.

But when had she ever cared what the matrons of Almack's or other places thought?

"Yes, yet there is more to live than that, my girl. Promise me you will think about what I've said. And perhaps humor me."

She gave him a smile, for how could she not? Her father was one of the most fair and honorable people she'd ever met. He never played favorites and always was the first man to offer help should anyone need it. "I promise to think over your words. However, to date, there hasn't been a man yet who's captured my heart." Inflamed her body yes, and she'd had fun sowing wild oats over the years—which had led to her horrid engagement—but once she found herself married, her freedoms would vanish as soon as her name changed. "I made that mistake with Colin. I was merely infatuated instead of in love. I don't believe my heart was in that relationship, and that is something I am not willing to repeat."

In fact, the man in question would need to set himself apart enough to capture her attention and her imagination for her to even give him a second look let alone a chance to win her heart.

"Understandable." He gave her a rueful glance. "Trust me. When the man who will change your life comes along, you'll know deep down, and your heart will clamor to tell you."

"I will take your word for it." The number of exceptional men she'd met could be counted on one hand.

"Oh, and there is one other thing I wished to ask of you."

She tamped down the urge to groan. "Oh?"

"It might prove interesting, but I've been asked to provide medical care at a bare-knuckle boxing bout tomorrow. You are welcome to attend with me if you'd like, just make sure you come dressed as a lad to prohibit any gossip that might get out. But it will provide you with the opportunity to dress wounds in the field and perhaps set a bone or two if you're interested."

How interesting! "Of course, I'll come with you. Though I think boxing is childish and reckless, it will be entertaining to watch the proceedings and perhaps lecture the boxers." Then she frowned. "As long as Colin isn't one of the competitors. If that proves true, I might wait in the carriage."

"I can't say that I blame you. The man's a bit thick in the head."

"I'd like to say it's a result of being hit with repetitive blows, but I think he's never been as bright as he wishes folks to think." Still, he'd been impressive enough in body that she'd given him a chance.

I won't make that mistake again.

Chapter Three

August 3, 1817
Elmbridge, Surrey
England

ALEXANDER FROWNED AS he surveyed the large clearing of grass where the bout would take place. Clearly, a meadow, and at one end, a handful of cows grazing on the grasses and wildflowers, but they seemed uninterested in the gathering of men into the once-quiet countryside. As the crowd of spectators swelled and formed a circle around the roped off section of ground that would serve as the boxing ring, his nerves crawled beneath his skin.

Why am I so damned anxious? It wasn't as if this was his first time fighting.

Since bare-knuckle boxing, especially for profit, was illegal within the bounds of London proper, most bouts took place outside the limits in the country. The sites were often farm fields, or clearings—even better—for sometimes thousands of spectators would assemble.

Since it had only taken a couple of hours to travel from London to the area where the bout was being held, there had been little to no fatigue from sitting in the carriage. Lewis had declined to accompany him and Duncan, and that was both a relief and an annoyance. What sort of brother didn't want to encourage another brother during a boxing match?

Especially when the winnings from the purse would be split between Alexander's personal coffers and the other half invested into the salon.

Assuming he would come out the victor.

"You look as if you will cast up your accounts," Duncan said to him as they stood by the carriage while assessing the area.

"Can you blame me? Look at the crowd," he said to his brother as a couple of men—no doubt sponsors of the event— walked a space of the clearing. One of the men checked the sturdiness of the posts that had been driven into the ground that secured the ropes of the ring. "Not as large as the crowd as if Lewis were fighting." His confidence wavered. "I'll disappoint them, won't I?"

"Indeed," Duncan said with a nod as he glanced about, then chuckled when he glanced at Alexander. "A few hundred here, which is not bad considering that it's a Sunday afternoon. If the wagering is frantic, all is not lost." He frowned. "Either way, you won't be a disappointment for the simple fact you are a Stapleton. How you measure your own performance is your business."

"Thanks for that," he said with heavy sarcasm in his tone.

"Battling nerves?"

"A bit, but they'll fade as soon as the bout starts."

"Good."

"Do you know who my opponent will be today?"

His brother shrugged. "I haven't been told, but I can check with the organizer—that rotund fellow over there—and find out." Duncan would act as his knee man tonight in Lewis' absence. This was the first time all the Stapleton brothers wouldn't be together for a bout, and that loss weighed heavily on Alexander's shoulders.

"Thank you. I could do with a few moments alone."

"Very well. I'll also try and build up excitement for you."

While Duncan was gone, Alexander leaned his back against the side of the carriage and closed his eyes. He concentrated on regulating his breathing, for the panic at not having Lewis there in support and encouragement made his chest tight. They had always been a team. What would he do without his older brother's hints and tricks in defeating his opponent?

Then the anxiety in his chest turned to a wave of hot anger. Why the devil did his brother care more about some woman who'd upended his world a month or so ago, instead of his brother whom he'd been with all his damned life?

"Alexander?"

He startled at the sound of Duncan's voice and popped his eyes open. "Yes? Is it time already?" Once more, his nerves crawled beneath his skin.

"Not yet, but I want you to come meet the doctor, the judge, and the referee." His wide grin immediately put Alexander on guard. "Also, I discovered who your opponent is. A Mr. Wilde from Liverpool. A big beast of a man, I'm afraid. Works the docks during the day, and a few nights a week he walks the floor at a gaming hell and tosses out men who make a noisy fuss."

"I see." It seemed luck wouldn't shine on him this afternoon. He cleared his throat and straightened his spine. "Let's have the introductions over with. The bout will start soon."

"Either try to have a fierce expression or a confident one. It won't do to portray such a gloomy persona in front of the crowd." Exasperation rang in Duncan's voice. "I am going to kick Lewis in the arse tomorrow for abandoning you."

"Ha. You can do so after I'm done with him." But Alexander allowed a tiny grin. "Newlywed aside, he should have been here."

"Agreed." Duncan led him over to a group of men standing inside the makeshift ring, talking to each other. "Gentlemen, this is Viscount Wexley, or rather Alexander Stapleton. He's the middle son of the famous bare-knuckle boxer, George Stapleton."

Interest lined the faces of the men assembled while the low buzz of conversation came from the gathering crowd. Each man introduced themselves, and Alex didn't pay much attention until it came to the doctor.

"It is good to meet you, Lord Wexley," the man said with an outstretched hand. "Dr. Tetford, and I very much enjoy bare-knuckle boxing, was a supporter of your father."

"That is good to hear." Alexander shook the man's gloved hand.

"I attended a couple of bouts last year when your older brother fought. Great boxer, that one, and I'm sure your father would be proud if he could see you now."

"Ah." No pressure or anything, to not only live up to his father's memory but also to Lewis. "Well, I appreciate your support. I hope I put on an entertaining show." Even though his nerves were more restless than before.

"There is no doubt that you will, and I'll be here if you need to be put back together." With a wink, Dr. Tetford ducked beneath the rope. "Best of luck, my lord."

Then Duncan came back to Alexander's side. "Come. The match will begin in half an hour. Best get ready and do some warmup stretches."

"Right." He nodded. "At least having something to concentrate on will steady the nerves."

Hopefully.

As they went beneath the ropes and headed to the corner that had been assigned to Alexander, the energy from the gathered crowd buzzed in his ears and filled his chest with confidence. He knew his skill level, and though it might not match that of his brothers, it was his and it was nothing to sneeze at, but still, he wished for the fight to begin.

"Woolgathering will see you pummeled out there," Duncan warned. The sound of his voice brought Alex back to the present. "You should be thinking about how to rout Pennyweather in as few rounds as possible."

"I know how to prepare for a bout." A hint of censure rang in his tone.

"I know that you do. Papa taught us well, but from what I've heard, this Pennyweather has some skill."

"At least it'll be a fair fight." Not that it mattered. Alexander would need to use every scrap of his strength to get through to the end.

"Rumor has it that he's been doing a stint in America, boxing in New York since his mother is from there."

"I am not afraid of an American. Loud, crass, and lacking in manners. Why would his fighting style be any different? Men like that make mistakes." Alexander shook his head to clear his thoughts. "Just want the bout to start." He stripped to the waist and handed his clothes to Duncan. Then he toed off his boots and tugged off his socks. There was a certain feeling of being grounded as he felt the coolness of the grass beneath the soles of his feet.

"Bloody Americans," Duncan whispered as he pulled a face. "A scrouge, to my way of thinking." As the knee man, it was Duncan's responsibility to see to his mindset, wellbeing, and water intake, to say nothing of offering him a knee like a footstool to provide a modicum of rest between rounds.

"Still, better than the French, I'll wager." Alexander shrugged as he wound strips of linen about his hands, which would help to cushion the blows. Duncan tied off the ends. "I'm as ready as I can ever be."

"Good to know. I hope since I haven't seen you in the salon to train much this week, all will be well."

Alexander looked at him with narrowed eyes. "I've trained. Mostly after public hours, for I don't like having anyone around."

"I can understand that. Sometimes, the extra noise is too much of a distraction." Duncan nodded, then peered at the opposite side of the makeshift ring where Alex's opponent and team were setting up. "Pennyweather is lean, but you've got more meat, and I assume power."

"Let us hope."

A shrill whistle blast pierced the air and scattered his thoughts.

Duncan blew out a breath. "Time to go."

A short, stout man stood in the middle of the boxing square and held up a hand. "We're about to begin." When the noise from the crowd died down somewhat, he continued, "Today's match is between a favorite boxer from London, the Viscount Wexley, but you know him as Alexander Stapleton." A roar erupted from the spectators. "And his opponent for this bout, the man who's worked his way through the American boxing circuit, Mr. Daniel Pennyweather." Another cheer rose from the crowd.

Clearly, they recognized the other man's name.

As the stout man gave a bit of a speech to thank sponsors as well as the boxers, Alexander moved his gaze over the crowd. At the edge, watching the proceedings, was a young man with a slouch-style cap and overly bright eyes. A hint of fiery red hair peeked out from beneath the cap.

"Look there, Duncan," he ordered in a whisper. "See that boy there? Does he seem too feminine for a male?"

"Put your head in the game, man," Duncan answered as he shoved at Alex's shoulder, but he followed his brother's line of sight. "What does it matter? Many women wish to attend boxing bouts, but they do so in disguise. Isn't that how Lewis met his wife?"

"Right. I guess it doesn't matter. Just odd, though. Best get to it, hmm?" After exchanging a glance with his brother, Alexander moved toward the judge in the center of the roped off ring.

Pennyweather came toward the judge from his side of the ring—a tall, lean man with blond hair arranged in a devil-may-care style and a heavy mat of hair on his chest that did nothing to hide how well defined his form was.

But that man wasn't him, wouldn't move like him. He had to believe that.

"Looks like I'll be able to put you down in two rounds, Stapleton," Pennyweather said with a fair amount of cockiness. "Rumors say you're not as skilled as your brothers, and the wagers say the same."

"I never listen to rumors, for they're usually twisted to the speaker's benefit." Alexander flexed his hands, then lifted his arms above his head and performed a few stretches. "Of course, I've never heard of you, so what does that say about your reputation?"

The other man sneered. "Don't try to confuse me with words. I'm here for the fight alone."

"As am I." Confidence and adrenaline flowed through Alexander's veins. Seconds later, he assumed his first position, fists at the ready, body taut and balanced, feet a shoulder's width apart. "Best of luck, Pennyweather. I'll try not to wreck your face too badly."

A whistle blast split the air. The judge shouted, "Remember, rounds will continue until one man is put on the ground and unable to stand after three seconds. Go!"

Alexander and his opponent circled each other, prowled through the meadow grass of the eight-foot by eight-foot roped off area. The judge as well as the doctor waited in opposite corners. How best to bring Pennyweather down? Anticipation rode his spine and anxiety pulled knots in his stomach, but he wanted to be the one to tag first. He threw the first punch. It connected solidly with the other man's cheek and threw his head back.

"Ha. Much like a bee sting. How disappointing." Pennyweather grinned as he struck out with a fast fist.

Alexander minced away, much to the crowd's roar of approval. "I'm just getting started, but wait until you see what else I've got." He swung a fist, but the other man dodged the punch while continuing to circle him.

"You'll go down so easy, I'll be able to enjoy a late luncheon." Pennyweather darted with a fast uppercut to Alex's chin that jarred his teeth together and caused him to bite the side of his tongue.

"Damn." Pain exploded through his face and the metallic taste of blood flooded his mouth, but he held his ground and returned a punch. Then they were into the thick of the first round as blows rained and fists pummeled, landing on solid flesh in rhythmic intervals. One of his jabs sent Pennyweather staggering backward, but the man recovered and came at him with fists flying. Alexander didn't give quarter. He defended himself with adequate ease and pounding fists.

Minutes ticked by counted by the dull thud of fists into bodies, fast footwork, and a few curses. Finally, his chest burst t and his lungs slightly burned before the round was called.

Grateful for the brief reprieve, Alexander plodded to his corner, as did his opponent. "Pennyweather is quite tenacious and has one hell of a right hook." He perched upon Duncan's knee as various portions of his body throbbed in pain.

"Then you'll need to do a better job of counteracting him." Duncan handed him a ladle of cool water from an oaken bucket. "Move your feet faster like Papa taught us. That is something Pennyweather doesn't do well."

"Right." Alexander wiped sweat from his brow with the back of his hand. After taking a deep sip from the ladle, he gave it back to his brother.

"You've gone against worse before." Duncan rubbed the muscles in Alex's shoulders and neck. "Wear him down, keep your jabs quick and fierce, and then try to nail him in the middle. I think I heard that he'd suffered broken ribs about six months ago."

"Good to know."

Another whistle blast announced the start of round two. Alexander returned to the middle of the ring to face off with his opponent once more.

"I've had about enough of you, Wexley," the other man growled. A cut on his high forehead glittered with dark blood. "I want that prize purse."

"So do I," he tossed back.

"Titled men like you have no need for the coin."

"In that, you are so wrong. Titles are often empty. Mine is no exception."

"You English nobs are all the same. Pretending to be something you're not to keep up appearances in society."

A hard uppercut to his jaw had Alexander staggering backward. He hadn't expected it. The crowd roared and as one entity they surged forward. Quite fickle in their support, it seemed, but then, people liked to see blood, and they enjoyed making coin on a wager. Pain exploded through his head, but he kept his feet. Reminding himself this wasn't some damned drawing room and there was no need for conversation, Alexander darted toward his opponent with a grunt. He landed two quick jabs to Pennyweather's stomach and cheek.

The man retreated before gathering himself and charging at Alex to once more exchange blows that were more like hand-to-hand combat than boxing.

Well, if that's what the man wanted, he'd have it. Again and again, Alexander drilled his fists into the other man's body, making certain to land them into either side of his ribcage, but the boxer wouldn't fall, even after a grimace of pain crossed his face.

Pennyweather got off a few good punches of his own, but Alex kept his feet through sheer stubborn determination, for he didn't want to disappoint his brothers or his supporters in the stands, damn the pain cycling through his body.

"Give it up, Pennyweather. I'm the better fighter." So saying, he delivered a swift right hook to the other man's cheek that had the other man spinning about. There was a moment when Alex thought the man might fall, but he didn't.

"I'm coming back for you in the next round." The man wiped at his brow with a hand that had bloodied knuckles, the same as Alex's.

"We'll see." Then the round was once again called without a clear victor. As he looked out over the crowds, his gaze landed on the doctor in one corner, but what took him by surprise was the young man in the slouch cap who stood next to him. When their gazes connected, he knew beyond a shadow of a doubt that person was a woman. As she gave him a tentative wave and a nod of encouragement, he frowned before stumbling back to his corner. Then he dropped onto Duncan's bent knee, panting. "The man is a plague," he admitted in a whisper.

"Most Americans usually are." Duncan plied him with water, and Alexander gratefully drank from the ladle. "But I saw him wince when you tagged his left side. Concentrate there."

"I'll try that, but he's uncommonly skilled." And damn, he didn't want to think about the bout right now. He stood, glancing once more at the woman in disguise who still stood at the doctor's side. When their gazes connected, she again offered a faint smile before a frown took it away. Heated sensation went through him from the brief exchange.

What the hell is wrong with me?

"Damn it, Alex, concentrate," Duncan hissed, and gave his shoulder a push, which refocused his wandering thoughts.

"Right." *I don't need a woman in any capacity.*

The judge blew his whistle again. The next round was imminent.

"Keep your head out of your arse, man." Duncan again slapped his shoulder. "Go put this man down, so we can take our winnings and return to London." He shoved him, and it propelled him to the center of the ring for round three.

"It's time to end this, Wexley!" Pennyweather came out in a rage, and he engaged Alexander in a storm of blows, jabs, and punches that left him reeling and breathless. "Nothing to say, *my lord*?" Sarcasm went through his voice when he said the honorific.

"Not to you."

When one of the bigger man's fists drilled into his abdomen, pain swamped him, had him doubled up with pain. Another blow caught him in the temple, and then Pennyweather caught him by the shoulders, ramming a knee into Alex's midsection. Apparently, they'd left gentlemanly rules behind.

"You'll pay for that." After taking a deep breath, Alexander came back using a quick double uppercut, one with each fist that found purchase in Pennyweather's chin and the left side of his ribcage. Then he followed those with a blow to the man's temple.

But his opponent only grunted. He didn't fall, but he did deliver a kick to Alex's stomach with the flat of his foot.

"Not exactly a punch, idiot," Alexander wheezed as he stumbled backward.

"It's a fight, Wexley, not a tea party," the other man said with a grin made ghastly with blood.

In the back of his mind and from what sounded like a lifetime away, a female cry of encouragement infiltrated his brain over the roar and cheers from the crowd. Was she a lover of the sport or was it him she cheered on? Then Duncan shouted for him to keep moving.

Footwork would win the day, just as his father had taught, but damn his strength was flagging. Straightening his spine despite the pain and fatigue, Alex blew out a breath and once more faced his opponent. "Is that all you've got?" he taunted the other man.

"Give up, Wexley. You aren't as skilled as your sainted father." Pennyweather chuckled as he circled. "Your brothers are twice what you are."

The words chipped away at his confidence. "Shut up." Every movement he made brought spikes of pain to different places in his body, but he entered the fray once more. "Either take your shot or concede the bout."

"To you? Like hell." The other man came on like a summer storm. He had strength on his side and perhaps fury.

Alexander defended himself as he'd been taught, but it was as if he were fighting a hurricane and being battered from all sides. Though he rallied a few times, punch after punch was exchanged, and Pennyweather didn't let up or give in.

As the match wore on, round followed round. Though he gave as good as he got, Alexander's strength wavered. His stamina waned. Blood dripped down his face from a busted lower lip and a cut on his forehead. He couldn't remember how many wounds he'd sustained. Sweat streaked into his eyes, stinging, and blurring his vision. The summer heat enveloped him enough that he was temporarily dizzy, for he needed water. His muscles burned from overuse. When would it end? At this point, he couldn't say. Though his body ached, he defended himself, for it was all he could do.

Then Pennyweather delivered a powerful blow to the left side of Alexander's head and temple. "You're done, Wexley, and I'll get to brag that I felled a Stapleton." His opponent slammed a fist into Alex's abdomen that sent him flying over the grass. "Leave boxing to the men who are much better than you," the man said as he peered down at him.

Alexander lay on his back while gasping for air and hurting from countless punches. Warning bells rang through his mind, and his conscience screamed at him to get to his feet, but his strength was shot. He collapsed into the sweet meadow grass and closed his eyes.

Eventually, the judge came near with the doctor, and he counted down from ten while Alexander didn't move. He couldn't bring himself to care that he'd been beaten by an American; he simply hurt too much.

"Mr. Pennyweather is the winner of today's bout!"

The crowd roared, for they weren't picky when it came to watching men pummel each other. Coming into the bout, Alexander had been favored to win, but the circumstances had turned on him, handing him a bitter defeat and allowing cold disappointment to lodge in his chest. When he opened his eyes, Pennyweather had walked to the center of the ring with the judge and referee holding up one of his arms each.

Some of the crowd swarmed to where Pennyweather held court, but Alexander couldn't spare any feelings for his opponent. Instead, he continued to lay on the grass until he could regain his breath and strength. For a few seconds, he let the darkness shimmering on the fringes have at him.

"Alex!" A gentle tapping on his cheeks brought him around. When he opened his eyes, it was to see Duncan peering down at him, but he wasn't alone. The redhaired woman he'd spied before knelt at his other side; she'd been the one to tap his cheeks.

Confusion gripped his mind. "What the devil?"

His brother snorted. "Viscount Wexley, this is Miss Lydia Tetford, the doctor's daughter. He sent her over to tend to you while he's busy with Pennyweather." He shoved a towel into his hand. "That wasn't your best bout, but not your worst," his brother murmured, but instead of the disappointment in the other man's eyes, there was a bit of worry. "How do you fare?"

"Not well. Took a fair beating out there." For the moment, he didn't look Miss Tetford's way else he make a fool of himself.

"In that last round, it seemed you were distracted. Why?"

Why did his brother need to be like this? "No idea." He refused to admit to being discombobulated from a wave by a woman, especially in front of her. Instead, he wiped at the blood and sweat on his face and head. "I need to train harder for the next bout."

Duncan scoffed. "You might be killed if you do another bout."

"I'll show you I can do better." And he would. He just needed to be more determined.

"Perhaps." His brother frowned. "I need to go make nice to some potential investors as well as to encourage interest in the salon."

"Work your magic, brother." As his brother left, Alexander lifted himself up on an elbow and looked at Miss Tetford. "Thank you for taking the time to check me over."

"It's the least I can do since you men will insist on being nodcocks by beating the stuffing out of each other." She tsked her tongue, and for the first time he discerned a water bucket by her side along with a smaller container of water and rags. "What you gain by doing that, I'll never know." The faintest hint of a Scottish brogue lingered at the back of her voice, and he rather liked it.

"It's in my blood. My father was a prize fighter."

"Oh, I am aware of that. *My* father can't say enough good

things about him." As she talked, she took a rag from the water, then set about to clean the dirt and blood from his chest and shoulders. "You took quite the beating out there. At one point, I feared for your survival."

"It surely wasn't that bad." With each swipe of the rags, her touch aroused him, or perhaps he merely enjoyed having someone fussing over him. Usually when women drifted near, it was because of Lewis' body or Duncan's handsome face and his charm. They didn't spare him—Alex—a glance, but then, his brothers weren't there. He gasped when she pressed hard on his ribs and then his stomach and abdomen.

"From what I witnessed, it was quite ugly, and I'm surprised you lasted three rounds." She certainly didn't guard her words, but that penchant for plain speech amused him. Then she leaned over him to clean up the wounds on his cheeks and forehead. "It doesn't appear you've broken bones, but you will look like a dog's breakfast on the morrow with cuts and bruises."

The faint scent of lavender wafted to his nose, and it took all his willpower not to touch her arm or even her cheek to see if her skin was as soft as it looked. "Such is the lot of a bare-knuckle fighter."

"Hmph." Then she offered him a ladle of water from the larger bucket. "Here. Drink. You need it."

"I'd rather have brandy," he said, as he accepted the ladle from her. When their fingers brushed, heat shot up to his elbow and he offered her a grin.

"You'll make do with water." Clearly, flirting had no effect on her.

It made him want to chase her all the more. After he'd drunk his fill, Alexander sat up, which put him even closer to her. Damn, but she was oddly distracting and quite pretty, even dressed as a young man. "What now?" The crowd milled about and Pennyweather had left the ring to greet his admirers. The doctor talked with the judge and referee as well as Duncan. As far as he could tell, none of the spectators lingered to talk with him.

Damned fickle men.

Her gaze flicked over his chest. "Get off the ground. You need to don your clothes and return to respectability." When she rose to her feet, she offered him her hand, and when he clasped hers, she tugged him upward with surprising strength.

"Thank you." Now that he was upright, the full scope of his injuries rushed over him. Uttering a groan, Alexander returned to his corner. He retrieved his lawn shirt from the grass and donned it, smoothing the garment down his chest. When he glanced at her, he frowned. "Why do you stare at me like that?"

"I am trying to weigh the consequences against the scandal," she said with narrowed eyes.

"Regarding what?"

"This." With a furtive glance about the immediate area, she then grabbed a handful of the shirt he'd just donned and swiftly pressed her lips to his.

Shock plowed through his chest, but before he could either return the gesture or reach for her form, she pulled away. But damn, those lips had been pillowy soft and tasted faintly of tea. "Why did you do that?"

Miss Tetford shrugged. "I wanted to. I've never met a boxer before, and I thought it would make me less angry with you and this silly sport if you were a good kisser."

There was much there he wished to question, but instead, he asked, "Was I?" Because he was curious, and this sort of thing didn't happen to him.

"Hardly." She snorted, but there was a wicked twinkle in her cornflower blue eyes. "I'm afraid I don't have enough information and it's too risky to continue to explore that here, but you are better at that than my former fiancé." She offered a bright smile. "However, I wish you well in your future endeavors, Lord Wexley."

"I beg your pardon?" Shocked again, he sat down hard on a tree stump. His mind spun, but it made him more than curious about her. She didn't answer, and instead handed him the socks and boots. Desperate to continue their conversation, he blurted, "If you wish to know more about boxing, come by the Stapleton Boxing Salon."

"Why? I find boxing far too reckless and bloodthirsty." She followed the statement with a frown.

He tugged on his socks. "So I can thank you properly for patching me up, and perhaps show you around. I'll do my best to explain and show you why boxing is a vital part of my life. Perhaps give you a lesson." Did that sound too impulsive or make him look as nervous as he felt?

"I will consider it. Until then, go home, my lord. Rest. Your body needs to recover." Then she left his corner and walked in the direction of where her father stood.

Alexander stared. What the hell had just happened?

Chapter Four

August 4, 1817
Stapleton Boxing Salon
Mayfair, London

L YDIA FROWNED AT the front window of what appeared to be a shoe seller, but above that shop was the Stapleton Boxing Salon.

What am I doing?

Yesterday, she'd attended an illegal boxing match in Surrey with her father, and even though she didn't enjoy bare-knuckle fighting or the crowds of bloodthirsty people only there to see two men pummel the stuffing out of each other, she appreciated parts of the aesthetic of it, but only when it came to Viscount Wexley.

Seeing him shirtless, which allowed his torso to show at full advantage as he moved, and his muscles working beneath the skin had caught her by surprise. She'd been breathless more than a few times even while silently berating him when he'd received blows and punches. Though he'd lost the bout and had ended it being temporarily unconscious, she came away impressed enough to kiss him.

Apparently, I went a bit insane yesterday. That is the only explanation.

Her views on having a man in her life hadn't changed, and

she still couldn't figure out why she'd felt compelled to kiss a stranger—briefly though it had been—but there was a bit of curiosity about the world he occupied, and that brought her here this afternoon, standing on the pavement in front of a shoe seller, staring at the windows of a boxing salon.

"Miss Tetford?"

Drat.

Lydia whirled around and frowned when she spied the younger Mr. Stapleton coming toward her. "Ah, Lord Frampton." At the last second, she recalled the title he'd used yesterday during introductions, when his brother had been unconscious and they'd met over his prone body. "How lovely to see you." With a bit of nervousness, she gripped the shoulder strap of her leather doctor's bag with more force than necessary.

He touched the brim of his beaver felt top hat that sat at a rakish angle over his left eye. As soon as he closed the distance, he asked, "What are you doing here? Frankly, you seem a bit lost." With a glance about the area, he frowned again. "Where is your carriage?"

"Oh." A bit of heat went through her cheeks. "I sent the driver home since I didn't know how long I'd be here or if I wanted to browse the shops after this visit."

"A visit to… the boxing salon? In skirts?" He sent his gaze up and down her person.

"Um, yes?" She ignored the continuing heat in her cheeks, for she hadn't thought about her attire. The day dress of striped cream and turquoise lawn wasn't exactly inconspicuous here, nor was the straw bonnet with matching ribbons. There was nothing for it, so she cleared her throat. "I thought to call on Lord Wexley and see how he's faring after yesterday's disastrous bout. He did take a rather hard hit to the head."

"There is that." With a faint grin flirting about his lips, Lord Frampton gestured with a hand. "Come. The rear door to the salon is in the alley. While our clients access the upper floor through a door inside the shoe seller, my brothers and I use the rear door, which accesses the office without needing to walk through the salon itself."

"Ah, and makes it more clandestine."

"Indeed."

In silence, she followed him around to the side of the building where an unassuming door waited. Once he'd tugged it open, she proceeded him and was immediately confronted with a narrow, wooden staircase. She ascended and on a small but tidy landing, she waited for the viscount to join her. There was just enough room for the two of them in front of a nondescript door, of which he unlocked with a tarnished brass key, and once he'd pushed the panel open, she went into the office he'd spoken of.

Venetian blinds at the plate glass windows that overlooked Brook Street were closed to shut out the afternoon sun, which gave the room a dim, intimate feel. Matching blinds at another window, this one interior and presumably looking out to what was the salon proper, had also been closed, but her gaze fell upon the man sitting behind the large oak desk. "Lord Wexley." The words left her throat without her authorization, and they sounded overly loud in the silence of the space.

He startled and then gawked as Lydia and Lord Frampton came around the desk to linger in the open in front of the office. Finally, he scrambled to his feet with a wince. Clad in tan breeches, a fine lawn shirt, a waistcoat of light green satin with a jacket of bottle green superfine that enhanced the breadth of his shoulders, he was the perfect image of a gentleman about Town.

"Miss Tetford?" Purple and black bruises decorated his cheeks and jawline on one side while another was barely visible on the side of his neck over his cravat. "What the devil are you doing here?" Then he slammed his gaze to his brother. "Did you have a hand in this?"

"Of course not," Lord Frampton said as he made his way to the door that would open out onto the salon floor. "I was coming to the salon anyway for my scheduled lessons this afternoon when I met Miss Tetford on the pavement. When I couldn't determine if she was dithering about going up even though she wished to check on your health, I showed her the discreet door instead."

"Ah." The viscount bounced his gaze between them. "Uh, as you can see, I am quite well."

She snorted. "That remains to be seen. Any man who willingly lets another man beat on him certainly isn't well."

Across the office, Lord Frampton snickered as he tossed his top hat and gloves to a nearby chair. Had the viscount told his brother that she'd kissed him yesterday? From all accounts, it didn't appear that he knew. "I have clients, so I'll bid you a good day, Miss Tetford."

"Thank you." Lydia nodded. Once the man left her alone in the viscount's company, she turned about to face him. "How are you feeling, Lord Wexley?" A bit of dark brown scruff clung to his jaws and cheeks while the thick brown hair on his head waved to the left in an intriguing swoop that had her wanting to run her fingers through those tresses. There was no doubt he was a handsome man, but she shoved that realization to the back of her mind. "Anytime a man is rendered unconscious from a blow, he needs to be monitored."

"While I appreciate that, I am quite well." Then he shoved the fingers of one hand through his hair, and she was obliged to tamp down on the urge to sigh with appreciation.

Get hold of yourself, Lydia. It is unseemly to want to melt into a puddle when faced with a man with lovely hair.

"At least let me give your head a cursory examination to set my own mind at ease." She moved to the desk and set her bag upon it.

"That isn't necessary, but thank you." An air of awkwardness brewed between them as he stood looking at her with questions in his hazel eyes. "Is that the only reason you decided to visit the salon today?"

"Not really. I came at my father's urging. He'd witnessed my tending to you yesterday in the ring and said that a good doctor would follow through with their patient after the initial trauma." Under no circumstances did she want to reveal that she was curious about him and the sport of boxing.

The viscount narrowed his eyes. "I might not be skilled in boxing—or rather winning bouts—but I do know when someone is lying to me." Slowly, he took a few steps toward her. "I can't give you a tour of the salon while we have clients on the floor, so I'll wager you're here for no other reason than you're curious. Either of boxing or of me."

"Impressive. It seems you're more than just a pretty face." It might have been the fact her imagination was spinning out of control, or he was just that arresting, but his presence seemed to fill the room. The scent of citrus and sage teased her nose as he came closer still. "If you must know, my answer is both. I *am* curious about you and this sport." Then she shrugged. "Since my father is a supporter of boxing, I might as well see what it's about, and why the Stapleton brothers are driven to succeed in it."

Interest lit his eyes. "Would you like a lesson? I can give you the first one at no charge, but don't tell my older brother Lewis."

"What would that entail?" As she glanced once more about the room, she saw a few tick mattresses stacked against the wall in a corner.

"Nothing more than some light sparring or showing you a few defense postures."

What would he say once he discovered she knew how to defend herself and that she was more than passable in basic jujitsu? Of course, that assumed she would continue this after one meeting. She wasn't quite ready to commit to anything, let alone friendship.

"I don't know…"

The viscount cleared his throat, then moved to an empty space in the office near the opposite wall where a pair of battered brown leather gloves hung on a hook. "Just one lesson, and while we indulge in that, you can tell me about yourself."

"Why do you care?" At least she'd be about to see him in

action again.

"Care is a strong word. Let's just say I'm curious as well."

One of her eyebrows rose. "About?"

"You. Not many women come to boxing bouts, especially disguised as young men."

Respect for him rose, for he hadn't hesitated in speaking what was on his mind. It was a refreshing change from other men she'd known. "There is that." She offered a smile while removing her bonnet. "My father invited me to accompany him to get a feel for what a boxing match was about."

"And to stitch up the opponents or set broken bones?" he asked with an elevated eyebrow of his own.

Heat went into her cheeks as she laid her bonnet on the desk. Then she removed her cream-colored spencer and draped it next to the headgear. "There is that. Unfortunately for me, there were no broken bones, but I suppose that's your fortune all the same."

"It is.

She came toward him while he donned the gloves. "I didn't know you used those to fight."

"I don't. These padded mittens are for sparring matches, mostly with clients who wish to learn how to box. Occasionally a bout will call for them, but it's bare-knuckle boxing for a reason."

"To apply impact."

"Yes." As he nodded, he beckoned her closer with a mitten-covered hand. "Today, however, it's to protect your knuckles, for you'll punch your fists into my palms." Then he winked. "A bit more difficult to do in skirting, I would imagine, but I'll wager you can manage."

Lydia snorted. "Tell me what to do."

"Very well. Stand in front of me with your legs a shoulder's length apart, knees slightly bent and raise your hands while curling them into fists."

Quickly, she followed instructions. "Is there a particular way to hold the fist that you Stapleton boys swear by?"

"No, just rest your thumb over your fingers instead of keeping it to the side of your fist. Everything needs to stay tight." When she did that, he nodded. "Boxers lead with their first two knuckles—the big ones—so aim with those knuckles and that is where your first will go."

"Right." This was very different than the defense she'd learned in the Japanese style. "Now what?"

The viscount raised his hands, palms toward her. "Punch my hands. Drill your fists into the middle, and use whatever force you wish. Nothing you do will cause me pain."

"You seem in enough of that already; you've winced three times since I've arrived." Then she moved and slammed her right fist into his left palm. The power that went through her body surprised her. "Oh!"

Wexley chuckled. "Ah, you didn't know you could feel that way, hmm?"

"I did not." When fighting through jujitsu, power came from using her brain and anticipating her opponent's actions, then using her own strength against the attacker. This was quite different. Power came from using fists as weapons.

"Keep going." He wriggled his mittens.

This time she drilled her left fist into his right palm. A thrill coupled with an odd rush of calm went through her. "By the way, you may refer to me as Lydia if you wish."

"A pretty name." The viscount grinned when she continued to rotate her fists into his palms. "I'm Alexander."

Somehow the name fit the look. She paused in punching his hands. "I come from a long line of healers. Currently, I want to be a doctor, but I am unable to be formally called that even after passing my exams due to one terrible fact."

"What's that?"

"I'm a woman."

He stared at her, but she couldn't read his eyes. "I'm sorry."

"That is the lot of a woman in this world, but that doesn't mean I can't continue to fight against it." And she slammed a fist into his once more.

Dear heavens, this feels amazing!

"Yesterday you said I didn't kiss as well as your fiancé. Are you engaged then?"

"Thankfully, not any longer." How to explain to him without making herself look bad in the process? "It was a bit of a misunderstanding, really."

His eyebrow rose again. "One that landed you a fiancé?"

Heat went into her cheeks. "I'll give you some background and you can decide." As she talked, she continued to drive her fists into his palms. "My mother was a Scottish healer; she knew all the lore and history of countless trees, shrubs, herbs, flowers, roots, grasses. Throughout my life, she provided the people around her with teas, poultices, salves, and all manner of things that would heal."

"That sounds helpful, and she must be where you got your hair," he said with another wink.

"It was." In that moment, she missed her mother, quite acutely. "Mama believed the gods gave us in the ground and sky what we need to heal. She was gifted but couldn't perform surgeries or set bones. That vexed her, obviously, but she knew when she should ask for help."

Punch, punch.

"When she married my father, who is an English doctor, they worked together for many years to heal all sorts of people. I admired the commitment and dedication of them both. How could I not want to become a doctor myself?"

"You have quite the legacy to live up to. I empathize with you on that. However, none of that explains the ex-fiancé."

"No, I suppose it doesn't."

Punch, punch.

"Out with it, Miss Tetford… er rather Lydia."

"Right." She paused in sparring, then blew out a breath. "A couple of years ago, my mother had some health issues. Pneumonia, and she died from complications with that."

"Ah, so she wanted you engaged before she left this mortal

coil, to have your future secured."

"Yes." She frowned as she nodded. "Even though she knew of my wishes to become a doctor instead of falling into the trap of domestic duties, which is how men control women." When she shifted her gaze from his mitten-covered hands to his eyes, she caught her breath to find an intensity there she hadn't seen before. "My father presented three candidates. I was forced to have dinner with them, meet them at routs and other social events when all I wanted to do was study my textbooks and finish the clandestine course work Papa had set out for me."

Punch.

"Only one man was compatible?"

"What can I say? I was naïve, and he was the lesser of the evils." Lydia shrugged. "Colin is a big Scotsman who has holdings near Edinburgh, which is opposite his blacksmith persona. He came into a bit of an inheritance and was considered a catch, so the match was made."

"What happened to make him a former fiancé?"

"Oh, a number of things, I suppose, which is too bad, for he was a decent enough lover." Why did she tell the viscount that? It didn't reflect well on her no matter how one looked at the story. When his eyes rounded with surprise, heat went through her cheeks. "I am not a skittish miss, you see, and I don't back down from a challenge."

"So I am coming to see."

"In any event, Colin has a bit of a temper. After all the charm and pretty words he fed me, he didn't take kindly to a fiancée wanting to be a doctor instead of an adoring wife and the mother of all the brats he wanted to have. Said he refused to have a wife of higher social standing than he."

Punch, punch!

"Clearly, you had no choice except to break the engagement."

"Exactly. That is not the life I want for myself."

"Being a wife and a mother isn't for everyone." He put the tip of one mitten beneath her chin and raised her head until their gazes connected. "There is no shame in that, Lydia."

The sound of her name in his voice sent an odd shiver of need down her spine. "I know, but society frowns upon women having dreams."

"Society can hang," he said, with enough conviction in his tone that she suspected he was often on the other side of proper more times than not.

"My father is a professor at the University of Edinburgh, but he was asked to be a guest lecturer at Cambridge for the coming term. So, not long ago, we moved to London where he has a few private clients that I help with. He rented a townhouse, and my brother Ian works with injured veterans in Town." She shrugged. "I said goodbye to Colin at Christmastide last year, told him we weren't compatible, that he could keep the dowry, and I would take the blame and whatever scandal followed." The heat of annoyance went through her chest. "He was livid, because he thought he'd have a well-heeled doctor for a father-in-law."

"As well as a way into English society, to say nothing of a pretty yet spirited wife who would bear him many sons?"

"Yes." How could he possibly put together a story so close to the truth? "I refuse to marry a man who wants to control every aspect of my life, right down to what I will wear or what I will do with my time. I might be a woman, but that doesn't mean I can't have dreams and goals for myself that run at cross purposes to everyone else's."

Once more, the viscount raised his hands. "No need to convince me. I can hear the conviction in your voice, but it also sounds as if you are hanging onto deep emotions you need to let out."

"Perhaps." She punched one of his hands. "I, uh… I don't have many friends to talk with or ones that I trust." With a huff, she blew back an escaped curl that fell over her forehead. "Besides, I excel at being in control. I'll be fine."

Punch, punch.

Yet how long could she continue being in said control without feeling as if she were shattering from everything? The engagement, the verbal abuse she'd taken from Colin, the scandal and bruising of her reputation from breaking the engagement, the disappointment from her father, not staying true to the promise to her mother, the thrill from studying and passing exams, the excitement gained from working on live patients at her father's clinic?

Perhaps Alexander was more attuned to her mood or the slight vulnerability or perhaps she had given him an unconscious invitation in her eyes, but whatever the catalyst was, he caught her hands in his mitten-covered ones, gently maneuvered them to the small of her back and held them there, and finally, he claimed her lips with his.

"Oh!" Her eyes widened as she stared into his, but when he didn't pull away, when he moved over her mouth with a determination and an intensity that gave her pause, a shuddering sigh escaped her, and she relaxed her body until he released her hands.

This kiss was much better than yesterday's. He was gentle but firm in his approach, and it sparked something deep inside her she'd thought she'd evicted long ago. It gave her a taste of an inner strength she admired, as did the band of his arms around her, and for one fleeting second, she knew a powerful urge to surrender to this man, let him hold her and shoulder some of the burden she struggled beneath, if only to allow her to breathe.

All too soon, the kiss was over, and the viscount pulled away. When he released her, he didn't sully the embrace with an apology, which she appreciated. In fact, he grinned, which prompted a grin from her. "Well, I have clients waiting and shouldn't linger here much longer, else Duncan will come bursting in." With his teeth, he tugged at the laces of the mittens until he was able to wrench them from his hands.

"Oh, of course. I need to get on with my day regardless." Shaking the confusion and bemusement from her mind, Lydia retrieved her spencer and then shoved her arms into the sleeves. "Uh…"

"Yes?" There was a twinkle in his eyes she didn't quite trust, but largely wanted to explore.

"I… I wouldn't mind continuing boxing lessons. After all, what can one truly learn from a first one? Besides, it's a good way of working off restless energy and helping to clear my thoughts."

"Excellent." Pleasure lined his face. "Come back to the salon whenever you'd like, or I can come to you if you'd rather not court scandal by coming here. Just send a note 'round. However, if you wish to have lessons here, they'll need to be before or after working hours, and you'll need to enter by way of the discreet entrance."

She nodded. "Thank you. I shall let you know what I decide." Then, still with her brain in a state of confusion, Lydia hurried across the office floor and out the door to the narrow landing beyond. Only after she'd gained the alley did she remember that she'd left her bonnet on the desk in the office.

Chapter Five

August 6, 1817
Stapleton Boxing Salon
Mayfair, London

"DAMN IT, ALEX, pay attention to what you're doing!"

The command combined with annoyance in Duncan's voice wrenched Alexander from his wandering thoughts just in time to see his brother throw down a pile of tick mattresses a few yards short of where they were supposed to go near the office window, for in multiples, they were rather heavy.

"My apologies." He blew out a breath. Already, the summer's heat was seeping into the boxing salon even at the hour of just ten past nine in the morning. "It seems my mind insists on darting about to things that don't matter."

"Like a redhaired woman dressed as a man who showed up at your bout the other day?" A knowing twinkle entered Duncan's eyes. He dragged the ticks over to where they belonged. It was where clients practiced bouts when in the salon. "The same one who had the audacity to kiss you on the field after the bout?"

So his brother had witnessed that? *Well, shit.* "What?" Alexander snorted as if the suggestion was beyond ridiculous. "I'd forgotten about her truth to tell." Under no circumstances could he have his younger brother sniffing around. "As well as that kiss. She initiated it, by the way. I had nothing to do with it." Except that it had thrown his life unexpectedly sideways.

"Ah, so then when she showed up at the salon the day after that to check your injuries and lingered in the office for nearly an hour?" Duncan continued shamelessly with an ever-widening grin. "That must have also been a one-off experience? And just what transpired between the two of you during that time?"

Heat crept up the back of Alexander's neck. "Nothing, I swear." He shrugged and then turned away to switch one of the straw-filled bags with one that had fresh filling. "She wanted to know how I fared with my injuries. I told her I was well enough and had to fend off an examination." By the time he'd noticed she'd left her bonnet behind, it was too late. She'd already made her way along the pavement, and he hadn't wanted to call her back in the event passersby would take too much interest in that. So he'd put it into the bottom drawer of Lewis' desk in the hopes he might see her again.

"And?" When Duncan came near to do the same with one of the sand-filled bags, expectation lined his face.

"Why do you think there's an 'and'?"

"There *always* is when a woman is concerned."

Well, Duncan would know, since he very nearly had a different woman on his arm every two weeks. "And then I offered a quick lesson in how to punch, which she accepted. During that lesson, she told me about the bounder she'd been engaged to and about how she'd broken said engagement."

"Ah. Do you think she'll become a regular client?"

"It's difficult to know. She doesn't share much, and only what she thinks someone needs to know, or at least I'm assuming that is so." He helped his brother drag the used bags to a back storage room where the interiors would be refreshed at some point in the week. "I suppose even a woman who broke an engagement could feel hurt, correct?" Or confused, angry, annoyed, unappreciated, especially if what she'd said about her former fiancé had been true.

Why wouldn't it be, though? Yet he didn't know her all that well.

"Your guess is as good as mine. I've never known a woman who would willingly leave an engagement." Duncan returned to the salon floor with Alexander in tow. He went for a pile of leather mittens that had been thrown haphazardly to the floor after use. "What else did the two of you talk about during her visit?"

"Not much, for there wasn't time." He omitted the kiss as he grabbed a couple pairs of mittens, then strung them onto a hook resting on the wall. "I assumed she had a previous appointment." Or considered her work done for the day after sending his world skittering into confusion and awe.

Before either of them could say more, Lewis came into the boxing salon.

"Good morning, fellows." He shot them both a bemused grin, and there was a red mark beneath his jawline. "I hope your morning has been as lovely as mine."

Alexander exchanged a glance with Duncan, who shrugged. "That largely depends. How have you spent your morning, and does that redness above your cravat mean there was overexuberant kissing or exploration with teeth involved?" It wasn't well done of him, but then Lewis had it coming for being absent much of the past month.

Ruddy color seeped up Lewis' neck and into his cheeks. "Uh, well, Cecilia and I were rather… amorous this morning and—"

"Stop." Duncan held up a hand, palm outward while shaking his head. "I do not want to hear about your carnal pursuits with your wife."

Lewis bristled. "Can I help it if I adore her?"

"You should go *adore her* somewhere else, and leave us out of it. Why haven't you gone on a wedding trip?" Alexander asked in some annoyance, for he and Duncan had just gotten used to doing everything by themselves without their older brother present.

"I didn't wish to abandon the salon," he said as he rolled his shoulders and then tightened the knot of his cravat. "Indulging in a wedding trip seemed ill-advised at this time, especially when we're gaining new clients every day."

"Ha." Hot annoyance rose in his chest. "What the hell do you think Duncan and I have been doing this last month when your attendance *anywhere* has been sporadic at best?" Unable to stand still, he strode into the back room, grabbed a broom, and then came back into the salon proper, for dust and dirt and other detritus needed to be swept off the hardwood. "We have been taking care of everything connected to the salon and sacrificing our leisure time in the process."

Duncan nodded, for it had been a continuing issue. "True. We don't begrudge you the wife, of course. It is your duty and responsibility as the earl. However, you could have at least attended Alexander's bout last week. Perhaps he would have made a better showing."

Damn. He'd no idea that Duncan would have brought that up, but now that the complaint had been lodged, what would their esteemed older brother say? Waiting with the broom stationary, Alex glanced in their direction.

"Right." Lewis nodded. He bounced his gaze between them. "I'd heard Alexander was largely unsuccessful at that bout." Then he frowned as his attention landed on him. "Did you forget all of your training, or did you largely give up out there in the face of a better opponent?"

"I beg your pardon?" Needing an outlet for his ire, Alex continued to sweep the floor. "My opponent was well-matched to my skill set. He was merely the better fighter, and since I didn't have you there to counsel me in how to move my feet or where to find his weaknesses, I went down hard in the third round."

Duncan nodded. "He was out cold for a few seconds."

Surprise went through Lewis' expression. "Did you sustain a head injury?" His glance went to Alexander's head.

"I don't believe so. My bruises are only just now starting to fade, but my mind is working like it normally does, and I haven't forgotten anything." That show of concern from his brother didn't negate the fact that he'd abandoned the bout for his own purposes. "What the hell were you doing that you couldn't attend?"

Another red flush rushed up Lewis' neck. "I was with Cecilia. Though I had every intention of attending the bout, time ran away and before I knew it, we were taking tea followed by other… things." He cleared his throat. "By the time my thoughts were my own again, the bout was over."

Duncan snorted. "So you decided bedding your wife was a better pursuit of your time than supporting your brother when he needed you the most?" He tsked his tongue while shaking his head as he finished hanging the mittens. "I remain conflicted on that, for I wouldn't pass on the opportunity for carnal relations either, but then, *I* was the one who was with Alexander at the bout, so there's that."

Of course, Lewis took that as an insult. He bristled and one hand curled into a fist. "Do not think to lecture me on what I should do with my life. It is difficult enough trying to navigate these waters myself and having Mama haranguing me still, without you boys piling on."

Finally, Alexander spoke. "Well, it doesn't matter now, does it? I lost the bout, and much of that was probably because the person who should have been my biggest support wasn't there." He shrugged, then finished sweeping the floor, using the copper pan to brush the dust and grit into.

Lewis shook his head. "No, you lost because you refuse to learn other tactics than what you already employ. Part of boxing is changing things." He stormed into the office, which was essentially his. Springs in the chair behind the desk protested as he dropped into it.

Was that true? Did he refuse to learn anything new? It was something to consider. "Regardless, the next bout I enter, I expect your arse to be there. That's how it's always been with the Stapleton brothers. Together."

"The next bout you enter, you're liable to end up maimed or

dead unless you train harder," came Lewis' retort.

"If anyone would know about that, it would be you," Alexander shot off before thinking. Not being able to fight in bouts for prize purses was something that Lewis still took to heart. Without that, he couldn't add funds to the Stapleton coffers, and it weighed on him.

Several minutes went by while Alexander and Duncan continued to put the salon to rights in anticipation of it opening for the day.

Then Lewis appeared at the door to the office with Lydia's bonnet hanging by its ribbons off a forefinger. "Would either of you want to explain what the hell happened in my office and why the deuce this was left behind?"

Well, shit.

Alexander shot a glance to Duncan, who shrugged. "Uh, I had a potential client come in unexpectedly the day after the bout. Not knowing her skill set, I had her punch fists into my palms as we discussed the possibility of making a schedule."

Lewis' eyebrows soared. "A her?"

"Yes." After Alexander replaced the broom, he crossed his arms at his chest. "What? You are the only one allowed to have a woman in this space?"

"Do you understand how scandalous that is?" Conveniently, Lewis ignored the question. He tossed the bonnet into the office, presumably in the direction of the desk, where it fell with a dull thud... somewhere. "Having a woman traipse inside the salon in, I assume, skirting?"

Before he could answer, Duncan inserted himself into the conversation. "To be fair, I encountered Miss Tetford on the pavement outside the shoe seller. She seemed a bit confused as to how to access the salon, as she was here to check on Alexander's injuries following the bout."

"So you led her into the salon after it had already been open?" Incredulity rang in Lewis' voice as he stared.

"Actually, no. I have more brains than that." Duncan glowered at their older brother. "I took her upstairs to your office by way of the discreet entrance. No one saw her enter, since the door to the salon was closed and your much-lauded Venetian blinds closed." He shook his head. "Alexander was inside the office, working on the books, so don't come the crab at either of us. At no time did the doctor's daughter leave the office."

"Why the hell did either of you even let her in?"

This is outside of enough.

Heated annoyance rose in Alexander's chest. "Don't blame us when you set the precedent." He narrowed his eyes at his older brother. "The second you allowed Cecilia inside the salon was the moment when it was acceptable for Duncan and me to go outside the norms of polite society."

Duncan chuckled. "As if I haven't been doing that all along."

"Do shut up," both Alexander and Lewis said together.

Still annoyed, Alexander continued. "Miss Tetford's motives were pure. She brought her doctor's bag and truly wished to examine my head to make certain I didn't sustain any further injuries during the bout."

"So, between that and the punching lesson, was that all?"

"Uh…" Heat seeped up the back of his neck. To cover that, he shoved the fingers of one hand through his hair. "If you must know, I kissed her." When his brothers gawked at him, he shrugged. "She is a fascinating person."

"Fascinating, eh?" Lewis asked with speculation in his eyes.

"Indeed."

With a nod, Alexander moved toward the middle portion of the salon floor where four tick mattresses rested in a line. Instruction occurred there, and the tick mattresses provided padding if a client was sent to the floor while fighting with their teacher. Toward the door two wooden structures that resembled a man's form waited, wrapped with linen and padded so a student could practice their hooks and jabs. Alexander punched one of the form's faces. If the features drawn somewhat crudely on one of the oval-shaped faces loosely resembled Lewis, there was a reason for that, and why this one remained Alexander's favorite.

Clearly, Lewis waited on a more in-depth answer. With a sigh, he continued. "As we were talking, I discovered that Miss Tetford wishes to become a physician."

Lewis nodded with a frown. "While that is aspirational, it is a dream that won't be fulfilled since women are not allowed to hold that position or even enter medical school."

"That hasn't deterred her, apparently, and since her father and brother are physicians, she has no doubt had access to medical textbooks as well as examinations, which she's passed under her father's tutelage."

"Impressive, of course." Lewis drifted over to Alexander's position with Duncan trailing behind. "I do have one question. Are you interested in her?"

Was he?

Stepping away from the punching form, he shook his head. "Not romantically. She's quite intelligent, and I appreciate that."

One of Duncan's eyebrows rose. "Then why'd you kiss her? Twice."

Lewis bristled again. "Twice?"

Damn you, Duncan. Alexander sent a withering glance at his younger brother, who grinned back like a loon. "The first one was started by her after the bout when she was tending to my cuts and bruises." Why the devil was he having to defend himself? "The second I claimed in your office when she came for a visit. As for the why?" He shrugged. "She was there."

Duncan clapped his shoulder and gave him a shake. "Any port in a storm, then?"

Laughter was exchanged between his brothers.

"Hilarious. Have a good jest." Alexander glowered at them both. "I'm not looking for a romance at this time in my life, and God forbid, not a wife. I have more conviction than you, Lewis, and do not want that sort of responsibility or expense."

"Ha." Lewis shook his head. "When the right woman comes along, you'll change your mind because you won't have a choice.

She'll come in like a storm and rearrange your thinking." He shrugged. "Whether it be fate, destiny, or just tugging at your heart strings, you'll topple, and then you'll finally understand how I feel."

"Well, thankfully, Lydia isn't like that. She has plans to be a doctor only and she's not going to deviate from that. Says she doesn't want to marry. I respect that."

"Lydia, is it?" Duncan said, then followed the insolent inquiry with a whistle. "Awfully familiar for a man and a woman who have no interest in each other."

"We are acquaintances that might be friends." This conversation was getting all too close and uncomfortable. Didn't the two of them have anything else to do?

Lewis regarded him with speculation. "Doesn't she interest you at all beyond friendship? I mean, let us be honest with each other. If you've shared a second kiss with her, she's clearly attractive, and there must be *some* sort of physical interest."

Another round of heat went up the back of his neck. "Right now, she is a potential client who wants to learn a few self-defense moves that might help her defend against an ex-fiancé if he decides to come after her. Or so I managed to extrapolate from our last conversation."

Duncan poked his shoulder. "Yet you kissed her."

"God, you're like a dog with a bone." Alexander frowned at his younger brother. "You of all people should know that kissing a woman doesn't necessarily mean anything. Perhaps I'm just an opportunist."

"And you're a liar," Duncan said with a shrug.

He blew out an annoyed breath. "How do you figure?"

"Well, you're not like me and chase any old skirt for the challenge of it, and you're not like Lewis, who apparently fell for the first woman who smiled at him, so what is your motivation for the kiss?"

Damn, it was a fair question.

"Honestly? I don't know." He glanced between both his

brothers. "I have never met a woman quite like Lydia before, and right now, I'm wary of her, don't know how to interact with her. She's a strong, determined woman, and while that is a bit intimidating, it also makes me extremely…" Pausing to search for the right word left him vulnerable to Duncan.

"Randy?" his brother supplied quite unhelpfully, with a wide grin.

"Lustful?" Lewis said as he piled on.

Briefly closing his eyes, Alexander huffed out an annoyed breath. "Yes, all right? All of that along with other things, but that won't matter, will it? Even if I wanted to court her—which I don't—she is not marriage minded. There isn't a point of furthering the connection, for I rather doubt someone as clever and intelligent as Lydia would consent to being some man's mistress."

Not that he wanted her to be that.

Did he?

Lewis exchanged a glance with Duncan before grinning. "Don't lose hope. It's early days yet, but I will caution you to not use the salon as your own personal love nest."

"Right, because you've already claimed it as yours, hmm?" Then he groaned when Lewis popped a fist into his midsection, not hard enough to leave a bruise but strong enough to make him pay attention. "Not fair."

"Everything is fair in boxing and love, brother. Remember that," Lewis said with a wink. "It'll make things much better."

"We'll see about that." Alexander returned the punch with a light jab of his own, and before he knew it, they'd moved to a training mat for a bit of impromptu sparring.

And for a few moments, it felt like it always had between him and his brothers, before Lewis married and before Lydia entered the scene to cause so much upheaval.

Chapter Six

August 8, 1817

L YDIA'S NERVES WERE unaccountably jumpy as she alighted from her father's closed carriage down the street from the Stapleton's Boxing Salon. She had sent a note 'round to Alexander at the salon yesterday asking for another lesson so he could have a contract ready to sign that would outline payment information.

After handing the driver a few coins, she gave him a faint smile. "Thank you, Giles. I shouldn't need a ride home, for I would imagine Lord Wexley will see me back."

"Of course, Miss Tetford."

With a nod, she watched him climb back onto his bench and then drive away, then she turned to face the façade of the building with a soft sigh. It was nearly the two o'clock hour, which was the time of her appointment, but since she hadn't come dressed as a young man—she'd forgotten and additionally, she wasn't comfortable going about Town in a disguise just because it was scandalous to be seen somewhere as a woman— she wondered which door she should enter the salon by.

In truth, Alexander promised he would be there to meet her, so she assumed they would enter through the discreet entrance, but as of yet, she hadn't seen him. When her father had asked after her plans for the day, she'd told him the truth: she was looking into the possibility of taking boxing lessons, for just that morning, she'd received another threatening letter from Colin, and what was more, he was in London.

Though she wouldn't admit it to her father, that fact terrified her. It also brought home how right she had been to terminate the engagement, even if the dowry had been lost. No doubt that extra coin was what had prompted Colin's urge to visit Town.

"Ah, there you are Miss Tetford."

She whirled about at the sound of *his* voice. He had just alighted from a hired hack, and after he paid the driver, Alexander came toward her. "Lord Wexley. How lovely to see you again." That wasn't a lie, for it had been a few days since she was last in his company, and once more she was struck by how handsome he was.

That brown hair that seemed to have a mind of its own when flopping over his forehead in what resembled a wave on the ocean made her fingers itch to see if it was as soft as it looked. Not even the jaunty tilt of his top hat on his head could hide that personality. The closer he came, the more his hazel eyes caught the sunlight which made them appear as clear and nuanced as a marble she'd once seen when her brother played with his friends. But what her attention caught upon was the breadth of his shoulders and how his jacket of bottle green superfine enhanced the whole of his torso. How well she remembered what he'd looked like stripped down to breeches in the boxing ring with those shadowed planes and the ridged abdomen.

What I wouldn't give to run my palms over that expanse.

Reminding herself that she didn't need a man in her life, Lydia forced a swallow into her suddenly dry throat. "I apologize it has been a few days. I'd meant to talk with you before about boxing lessons, but my father's patients all developed acute conditions at the same time, so I was obliged to assist him with their care."

"Never apologize for helping a person in need." With a grin, he gestured her toward the alleyway. "Please, come with me. We'll go up to my brother's office like Duncan showed you before. I can't remember how many clients and members are in the salon this afternoon, but we'll stay in the office to protect your privacy."

"Thank you. I appreciate that." In silence, she followed him, and when they climbed the narrow wooden stairs, she couldn't help admiring the tautness of his arse or how the muscles in his thighs played with each tread he took.

Get hold of yourself, Lydia! You have seen many other attractive men before.

At the landing, she stood beside him while he fished about in his waistcoat pocket. When he frowned, he patted himself down, and her gaze went to his mouth. Had his lips always seemed so sensual? "Damn."

"What?" It gave her something to focus on.

"I've misplaced the key to the door, and now that I'm thinking about it, I left it on my bureau top."

Did that mean her lesson today would be postponed? How annoying. A huff of annoyance left her throat. "How are you this irresponsible, especially since you are the one who keeps the books?"

He slowly turned to face her. "Can I help it if I've been somewhat distracted of late?"

"With what?"

"Many things, I suppose, but mostly wondering if I should enter another bout."

"Ah." Lydia couldn't help but point her gaze briefly to the heavens. "After your horrid showing at the last one?" When he stared, she snickered. "A glutton for punishment, are you?"

"Well, I, uh…" The emotions on his face went from shocked to annoyed, then to embarrassed. "That is to say, I'm a boxer at heart. Doesn't matter—much—if I don't win them all… I think."

Taking pity on him, Lydia laughed. "Don't take offense, Lord Wexley. Not all the Stapleton brothers can be prizefighters."

This time his expression landed on annoyed, and that emotion reflected in his eyes. "That might be so, but I need the prize purses."

"Why? Do you have vices that demand payment? A mistress, perhaps?" Though she enjoyed needling him, it was a good way to discover if he had a woman in his life.

"No." A red flush went up his neck and above his cravat and collar. "The truth?"

"That would be preferable. I have no time for dissembling, and lying doesn't endear anyone to me—male or female."

He nodded. "I need to build up a decent income to appear more attractive to women. In the event I'd like to potentially court one," he added in a rush.

"Oh." That was… surprising. And the fact he'd said it made him rise in her esteem. "Is that something you wish to do? Court a woman?"

"I don't know. Truth to tell, I'm confused about it." He shrugged, and his rueful expression pulled at her chest. "Ever since Lewis married, and with Duncan always having a lady on his arm at society events, I've been feeling left out, like on the outside looking in."

"While I hesitate to tell you this, I do understand what you mean." She leaned her back against the wall since the landing was crowded and his presence filled the tight space. "Many of my friends have married and are having children, and while it's not something I'm willing to entertain for myself just now, I've also learned that envy or jealousy is not a good reason to court or marry." When she met his gaze, questions clouded the hazel depths. "Those emotions are not the ones on which to build a relationship, and they might lose you the woman."

"I can see how that might be possible. Additionally, it might cause her to break trust."

"Exactly. Once that trust is lost, it is very difficult to retrieve."

For the space of a few heartbeats, silence reigned between them. "What if I find a lady that I *do* have an interest in, but because of my financial situation, I'm not at a point where I can offer for her. Should I ask, even if I thought I could grow to love said woman, and hope those feelings were truth and might be returned?"

"Oh, dear, such a complicated situation." Did that mean he had a lady in mind and needed the advice of another woman? She played with the strings of her reticule. "This seems as if it's a quick decision. Is it imperative that you find a wife immediately?"

"No, I suppose not."

"Then why are you trying to rush the timeline before finding the right fit?" When he remained silent, she blew out a breath. "I speak from experience, Lord Wexley. I rushed into an engagement due to my mother's wishes, but that match wasn't the right one for me and wouldn't have worked for the lifestyle I wish to pursue."

"Perhaps it *is* complicated." He shrugged, and once more her attention was arrested by the breadth of his shoulders. "My father didn't leave the family well off, and with Lewis unable to box any longer and Duncan being cut off from receiving funding from the family coffers, we desperately need the cash. Additionally, I am letting my rooms, as well as employing a valet and a part-time housekeeper."

That sent a frown tugging at the corner of her lips. "So, then, you want an heiress. You'll have access to her fortune as well as the time to sort your feelings." She couldn't keep the sarcasm from her voice. "Isn't that how the *beau monde* acts? Coin makes everything better, even matches that are ill-fated?" Was that truly the kind of man he was? Willing to sacrifice his heart on the altar of coin?

"Not necessarily. I'm only saying—"

"Oh, what an idiot." After muttering that, Lydia closed the short distance between them, stood on her toes, and then pressed her lips to his. Immediately, a rush of buzzing feeling went through her veins, but all it did was enhance the craving for more. Before she could really begin to enjoy the kiss, he pulled away without once putting his hands on her.

Surprise reflected in his eyes. "Why do you keep doing that?"

"This time was to stop you from talking and making more of a fool of yourself than you already are."

"Ah." He peered at her as if he couldn't quite puzzle her out. "Since this is the second time you have initiated a kiss, does that mean you enjoy doing so with me?"

Did she?

That one they'd shared in the boxing salon office still had the power to send tingles of need down her spine. In this as well, there was no purpose in lying. "I rather might, but more research is needed." Would he think her too fast or even too forward? "You see, I've never been good at being a passive miss waiting around to have someone take notice of me."

"No, I can see that about you. It must be the Scottish blood." A wide grin curved his lips. "That being said, I'm happy to oblige." When he reached out and then tugged her into his arms, she made no protest, and when he settled her into his arms and kissed her, Lydia couldn't help but shiver with the thrill that went over her.

Though he started slowly by moving over her lips as if he were introducing himself to her through physical touch, the moment she layered herself against his chest and looped her arms about his shoulders, the embrace heated as if a match were set to tinder.

When she uttered a moan of approval or encouragement, the viscount pressed her back against the wall, trapping her between it and his hard chest. The hint of an evening shadow on his cheeks and upper lip enhanced the sensations he imparted by claiming her lips or drawing the tip of his tongue over them.

As he probed their seam, she immediately opened for him, let him deepen the embrace, and she joyfully fenced with his tongue as they dueled for dominance. Heavens, but it had been a year or so since she'd last had any sort of relationship with a man, and kissing this one brought out a wealth of sensations that danced over her skin and through her blood. It revived the longing for physical touch, to allow a man access to her body merely for the pleasure that would bring, had an acute need to indulge in scandal that she'd buried for so long since she first gave away her innocence a few years before to one of the footmen in her father's employ.

"Alexander…"

"Mmm?"

"I need more," she whispered against his lips, wanting to continue chasing that high.

"As do I." The man took direction well, for he lost no time in cupping her breasts, and once he did, he worked the nipples into stiff peaks through the fabric of her day dress.

A soft moan left her throat, for that pleasure was enough to make her feel as if her feet were leaving the ground. With the slightest pressure of her gloved fingers at his nape, she hoped to encourage him to continue.

"Well, I hadn't expected to come upon this charming picture, but this is not the time nor place."

"Shit," Alexander breathed as he wrenched away from her. Shock shadowed his eyes as he glanced from her to the man coming up the narrow stairs. "You could have warned me, Lewis."

"I could have, but where's the fun in that?" Behind him on the stairs was a woman Lydia had not seen before who was dressed like a young man in breeches, shirt, and waistcoat with slouch-style cap, much like what she'd worn to the boxing match last week.

How interesting.

The woman spoke as she took in the damning scene. "I should probably go home."

"No, don't." Alexander cleared his throat, and even though it was now terribly crowded on the tiny landing, he acted as if he were in a drawing room. "Miss Tetford, this is my brother Lewis, or rather the Earl of Lethbridge, as well as his wife, the Countess of Lethbridge. As a matter of fact, he owns the salon."

To her credit, the countess waved. Amusement danced in her eyes. "Please, call me Cecilia." Her smile immediately put Lydia at ease. "Why are you and Lord Wexley out here?"

"He misplaced his key."

"Ah." The earl chuckled as he glanced at his brother. "And to pass the time, you decided to violate a doctor's daughter?"

Well, that was rude. Lydia frowned. "I'm nearly a doctor in my own right; I just don't have the certificate."

"Don't come the crab, Miss Tetford." Lethbridge waved a hand. He quickly unlocked the door and ushered them all into the office. "Does this mean the two of you are courting?"

Before Alexander could answer, she huffed. "We are not. That was merely a kiss."

"A *scandalous* kiss," the earl rejoined.

"Do hush, Lethbridge," his wife said with a smile. "I remember those days."

Alexander snorted in derision. "As if they were so long ago? You only met my brother just under two months previously."

"That's enough." Ruddy color rushed into the earl's face. "In any event, my wife wished to come by the salon so we could do some sparring."

Now that *was* interesting. "Ooh, that sounds fun. I wouldn't mind indulging in such exercise."

The Stapleton brothers exchanged uneasy glances. Finally, Alexander shrugged. "You've only had one lesson, and that wasn't truly sparring. Only punching."

She popped her hands on her hips, and her reticule smacked against the outside of her thigh. "Are you implying that I won't be able to hold my own?" She could have him on his back on the mats in a twinkling from her Japanese combat training.

When the viscount looked her form up and down, she tamped down on the urge to shiver, for it felt as if he'd run his hands over her body. "You are hardly dressed for sparring."

There were entirely too many people in the office. Heat swept over her person. Why wouldn't they open a window? "I can undress to my unmentionables or tie my skirting between my legs if stripping to a state of undress bothers you."

A flush rose up Alexander's neck. "Uh, that won't be necessary. Perhaps we can have a lesson some other time."

"Nonsense." The earl took command, clearly enjoying his brother's state. "Miss Tetford can spar in her dress. It's just the family here. We can have tea afterward."

Lydia nodded. "That is acceptable, Your Lordship. Thank you."

"Call me Lethbridge."

Then the countess linked their arms. "Before we start, let me show you around the space." But she looked at her husband. "That is if there are no clients on the salon floor?"

Alexander cleared his throat. "I believe Duncan has a few, plus walk-ups."

"Ah, well, we can do that another time, then, but Lewis is so proud of it, and he is a wonderful manager." She pulled Lydia to the windows that overlooked Brook Street. "In the meantime, we can let in some fresh air."

As they did that, Alexander guided his brother to the door that led to the salon. According to his facial expressions and the tight way he held his body, he was in a temper with the earl, so she strained her ears to overhear their conversation.

"What the hell, Lewis?"

"What?" To the earl's credit, he did seem confused.

"Why are you talking about courtship? You already know Miss Tetford isn't one for marriage," he hissed while jabbing a forefinger into his brother's chest.

Lydia's eyebrows went up. Had they previously discussed her? In what context? She bit her bottom lip, for she didn't know how she felt about that.

"Does that mean you're interested in perhaps pursuing such a thing with her?" Though the earl had a few inches on his brother and was a bit wider in the chest, Alexander stood his ground. It was obvious the two of them argued and got into each other's spaces frequently.

"To be honest, I'm not interested in anything except getting beneath her skirts."

Lydia glanced at the countess, who shrugged but couldn't quite tame a smile even if her cheeks blazed red. "What a prick he sounds like," she whispered to the other woman.

"Oh, I don't know. There is something lovely about a man who knows what he wants without being too wishy-washy about it."

"True." Was he the same type as her former fiancé? Surely not. She'd seen enough of him to know that already, but then, she wasn't averse to the idea he'd proposed, if evidenced by that kiss on the landing. Though she didn't want a marriage, she wasn't opposed to a tryst here and there.

Especially if it would gain her another peek at that fine physique of his.

"Behave yourself," the earl demanded in a fierce whisper. "Our family doesn't need any more scandal attached to its name."

"Ha!" Alexander shook his head. "*You* started the scandal."

"And I'm saying don't add to it," the earl growled as he wrenched open the door. "I'll go and find out when the salon will be free." He slammed the door behind him.

With a sigh, Alexander turned to glance at her. "In the meanwhile, I should be happy to teach you the finer aspects of sparring here in the office if you're of a mind? And then perhaps you could spar with Cecilia?"

Both she and the countess agreed, and she lost no time in removing her spencer and bonnet. "Please don't let me forget my other bonnet. I'm rather fond of it," she said as she deposited everything on the desk. "I've looked forward to my next lesson." It wouldn't end as she might have hoped, but there would be other times alone with the viscount.

Chapter Seven

August 9, 1817
Stapleton Boxing Salon
Mayfair, London

W*HY THE DEVIL am I here with ledgers as my only company?*

It was a Saturday night, and in the days before Lewis had married or before they'd opened the boxing salon, he and his brothers would prowl through society events in the evenings with no particular intent in mind except to discover which of the ladies might grace their beds once the clock struck midnight.

But tonight, he was in the office of the salon, totaling columns of numbers in the candlelight with shadows creeping in at the edges of the golden illumination because he'd had too many distractions. And he was only passable at the task of accounting, while Duncan was probably off doing wicked things to one of the many women he'd managed to charm this week.

Lucky bastard.

As the carriage style clock on the edge of the desk softly chimed the nine o'clock hour, Alexander paused with his pencil lead barely touching the paper. One of the biggest distractions he'd wrestled with this week was Lydia Tetford. Yesterday, after that kiss on the stairs outside the office, he honestly thought he might not survive the hour let alone a boxing lesson with her. As it had turned out, with his brother there along with his wife, nothing else of a carnal nature happened, and that left him frustrated.

And all he could think about was how much he wanted her.

God, the whole thing is impossible.

After tossing the pencil onto the open ledger, he shoved his hands into his hair. How had he had the unfortunate luck to find himself semi-involved with a woman who wanted no part in courtship and eventually marriage? It didn't matter that she challenged him on every level, nor did it matter that he craved spending time with her, for she walked a line between surrender and domination. How damned arousing was that? But if he chased after her and eventually somehow convinced her to let him bed her, what was the point of that? Yes, a tryst sounded appealing in the short term, but did he want that or was he truly hoping to chase something more?

Do shut up, Wexley. You haven't the funding to offer a woman a decent future, so the point is quite moot.

There was that, of course. And someone of Lydia's caliber would never fall for a man like him, especially when she knew of his precarious perch financially.

What if I'm not looking for love? If he couldn't pursue her with marriage in mind, did he dare offer something else without risking offending the hell out of her?

The whole thing was a bothersome coil.

When the public door to the salon swung open, Alexander's head came up. He looked through the windows out onto the salon floor with a frown as a man stood in the middle of the space with confusion written on his face. With a growl of annoyance, Alexander stood up from the desk, made his way through the office, and then entered the salon itself.

"May I help you?"

"Ah, yes." The younger man came toward him with an envelope in his gloved hand. "I first went by The Albany looking for a Lord Wexley, but he wasn't there, so the sender of the missive told me to try the Stapleton Boxing Salon."

His frown deepened. "You are searching for me?"

"Are you Lord Wexley?"

"Yes.

"Then this is for you." He offered an ivory envelope. "It was given to me with instructions to deliver it posthaste."

Who the devil would have sent this? Knots of worry pulled in his gut as he accepted the envelope. "Do you wait for a reply?"

"I don't. The woman who sent it said that hopefully you would come ahead of a message."

Intriguing and somewhat concerning. "Ah. Thank you." Alexander dropped a few coins into the man's hand. "Enjoy the remainder of your night." Once the courier left the salon, he ripped open the envelope."

The missive was short and to the point, just like the writer— Lydia.

A,

Something untoward has happened. My father is attending a rout sponsored by a man high on the instep with the league of London physicians, and I currently don't know where my brother is, for he isn't attending to patients at his clinic, so I'm turning to you.

Not to put a fine point on it, I was attacked by Colin, my former fiancé. He tried to win me back by mauling me while telling me that he didn't accept my refusal to marry him. He has been belligerent about that before, but only in letters. Now it has escalated into physical badgering. I managed to get away from him with a few well-timed kicks, but I'm frightened and suffering from reaction. Both of which have never happened to me before.

Please come when convenient, but even if it is not, I would like you to call all the same, for I don't want to be alone.

L

Alexander stared at the letter as first shock went through his system followed by hot anger.

What the devil? *She's been attacked?*

Then his protective instincts kicked in. I'm going to pummel the man into the ground. He didn't think, he just jumped into action. She needed him, and he would be there for her. Swiftly locking the door, he darted back into the office. Barely slowing down to grab his hat and gloves from the desktop, he blew out the candle, went out the rear door, cursed out the key when he fumbled in the process of locking the mechanism. Finally, he pelted down the narrow wooden stairs at a reckless pace. With his pulse pounding in his ears, he ran down the pavement for a block or two until he found a cab for hire. It was faster than summoning one of Lewis' vehicles from his mews.

On the short ride over to Grosvenor Square—and thank God the driver knew where Dr. Tetford and his daughter resided, since it wasn't something Alexander had discussed with her—his mind spun in a hundred different directions. What sort of man stalked a former fiancée and then went on to attack her?

Oh, he would pay, and dearly.

By the time he arrived at No. 16, he itched for a fight, if only to relieve the feelings of restlessness zipping through his veins. His rap on the door was immediately answered by a butler who showed signs of anxiety and worry.

"Please, follow me, Lord Wexley. Miss Tetford is in the rear parlor," the older man said as he led Alexander along the corridor. "The servants are all very concerned for her; she arrived in an alarming state."

"I can well imagine. When did she come home?"

"Nearly an hour ago."

"Right." He nodded. Shadows crept along the walls as he passed framed paintings depicting calming countrysides and seascapes. Obviously, the staff was preparing to put the household to sleep. "Has Miss Tetford ordered tea? If not, I'd like to do that before you retire for the night."

"Oh, yes, my lord, perhaps ten minutes past. However, she has asked to be left alone except to receive you. I trust you will protect her until her father returns?"

"I will." Alexander again nodded, for he was anxious to see her with his own eyes. "Perhaps leaving her be is best until I can get her calmed down. I would ask that you respect those wishes and if we have need, we will ring for you or a maid."

"Of course, Lord Wexley. Here we are."

"Thank you." As soon as Alexander entered the parlor, the butler closed the door. Immediately, his gaze went to her. "Lydia?"

Dear God.

"Alexander." She stood peering at a curio cabinet across the room but turned when he said her name.

Her hair looked a mess and bits of it had escaped the pins. For whatever reason, her bonnet hung on her back; perhaps she was in such a state she hadn't removed it even though she'd taken off the spencer, for it was on the floor in a heap. One sleeve of her jonquil-colored dress was torn, and the skirting had been smudged with dirt. She glanced at him with wild eyes, the green depths reflecting fear and confusion in the dim illumination of the one candle burning in a holder that had been set on a low table next to a tea service on a silver tray.

"I'm so glad you came. I didn't want to be alone and had no idea who else to ask." With that, she flew across the room and surprisingly threw herself into his arms.

With gladness, he wrapped them around her. "How do you fare?" he asked in a soft whisper as he held her. It seemed the right thing to do.

"I am quite out of sorts," came her reply that sounded laden with tears. That was something he hadn't witnessed from her before. When he tried to pull away, she wouldn't let him and held onto him all the tighter. He patted her back, encouraged her head onto his shoulder and hoped he'd indicated with those actions that he wouldn't leave her. "Tell me what happened.

Where were you when Colin found you?"

"I had finished my rounds at Ian's clinic—he's my brother—and decided I wanted to do a bit of shopping after since his place is close to that district."

He nodded. "That sounds like a lovely way to spend an hour." While he spoke, he ran a hand up and down her spine in the hopes of soothing her.

"I thought so too, for there is a new fan I'd quite like to have, but before I could enter the shop, I was hailed, and when I turned to see who it was, I saw Colin. It was too late to bolt, and in my shock, I'm afraid I just froze."

"Understandable."

She kept her arms tucked between them, resting on his chest, and he rather enjoyed the warmth of her. The scent of lavender teased his nose the longer he held her. "I told him in no uncertain terms that I didn't wish to see him or even talk to him, but he was having none of it. When he reached out for my arm, I dodged him the first time and edged my way down the pavement, but he came after me." A few sniffles followed, yet she didn't raise her head.

"He's quite the bounder."

"You have no idea." Finally, she pulled slightly back and met his gaze. Tears made her eyes luminous, and in that moment, she was the most beautiful woman he'd ever seen. "I thought if I could cross the alley and gain the pavement on the other side, I could reach the hack stand, but he caught my arm, tore my sleeve even through the spencer. Demanded that I talk to him because he wasn't going to accept the break of our engagement after all."

"You needn't continue if you don't want."

"I must, though." A tear fell to her cheek. "He is much larger than me, so he dragged me into the alley. The sun's rays didn't fall between the buildings, and it was a bit too dark for my liking. His hands were on my shoulders, and he shook me, made me look him in the face." She shook her head. "There has never been a more stubborn Scotsman, Alex. He demanded that I give him another chance, even though I've told him time out of hand we didn't suit."

"I think I can puzzle out what happened next."

"Then you would be quite wrong." At least she gave small chuckle. "Though he pounced, had the audacity to try and kiss me, I grabbed his arm, went into a defensive posture, dropped my hips, and then threw him over my back." When Alexander's eyebrows rose, she nodded. "I know the basics of jujitsu, you see."

But clearly, he did not. "That is a story for another day."

"Oh, yes." She nodded. "Barely had Colin gained his feet when I delivered a side kick, planted the flat of my foot into his midsection, and that put him back on the ground, allowing me to run away, and I didn't stop until I arrived home… except there is no one here. But I made certain the doors were locked, not that such a thing would stop a man like Colin. I'd forgotten my father had plans tonight, and as for Ian, I've no idea where he is, but he deserves leisure time without having to look after his sister." When her voice caught, his chest tightened.

"Did he threaten to come back?"

"No, but I wouldn't put it past him." As she spoke, Lydia's gaze dropped to his cravat, and she fussed with the folds of that garment with her fingers. Her breathing was calmer than it had been when he'd arrived. "When his letter campaign didn't work, he came to London."

"I'm sorry." Though the emotions she'd shown him were a bit out of character for her, or at least the strong façade she'd given him before, he liked that she shared more about her history as well as let herself be vulnerable in front of him. "If you'd be interested, I'm available to find Colin and clean his clock."

She once more met his gaze. "That isn't necessary, but I *am* frightened, and I don't like that feeling."

"It's completely natural, though."

"I am well aware of that. Once again, a man thinks he can coerce a woman into bending to his will, and that makes me angry."

"Brings out the Scottish in you?" he couldn't help but tease.

Her lips twitched, then she gave into a small laugh. "It does. My father always warns me that my temper will be my greatest downfall."

"It might, and honestly? I look forward to seeing you unleash the full force of it on someone… as long as it's not me." Alexander rested his hands on the curve of her hips. "For what it's worth, I empathize with you. The world isn't fair. Not all men are like Colin, just as all women are not gold diggers or title seekers. I am sorry, just the same, that you are in this mess. You don't deserve that."

"I'm sorry too."

He nodded. "You needn't go through this alone; I am here with you, and I won't let that man, or any other, hurt you further." Every word of that promise he meant.

"You are a good man. I appreciate that." She continued to hold his gaze. "Thank you."

"It is my honor." Suddenly, he wanted to be the only man to have the right to protect her, to defend her against whatever ill she might face, and even though the idea was ridiculous given that they had only just met and that neither of them wished to cultivate a permanent relationship, he couldn't help but persist in thinking it. "Just know you aren't alone."

There was no way to tell who moved first, but seconds later, their lips came together and she was more firmly in his arms, and they were kissing intensely as if the world would end tomorrow.

"Alexander?" She peered up at him, and with her green eyes framed with moisture-spiked lashes, every scrap of willpower he had eroded at the edges.

"Hmm?" Interest shivered through his shaft and hardened it. Purely madness to feel such desire for a woman he hardly knew, but there were stranger things.

Perhaps.

Lydia pushed at his chest. "Go lock the door." She manipulated the ribbon box at her throat. Seconds later, her bonnet tumbled to the floor. Then she removed her gloves.

Surprise filled his chest. "Why? Your butler said you'd already told him you didn't wish to be disturbed."

"I know that, but now I *really* don't want to be disturbed." Her eyes widened, and he'd be an idiot not to understand her unspoken meaning or the need shadowing those green depths. "It might be a reaction from what happened earlier, or merely a continuation of the kiss you and I shared from yesterday that was interrupted, but I would like to do more with you than kissing… if you're of a mind?"

"Oh… I…" To hell with trying to figure out what it all meant. If she consented, so did he, and her desire fed his own. "God, yes I am."

With a grin, he rushed across the room to do her bidding, and damn if his hand didn't shake as he turned the key in the door. Afterward, he took his own gloves off and tossed them to the floor, not caring where they landed. On his way back to her, Lydia met him in the middle of the room, curled her fingers into his lapels, and reeled him in for another kiss. This one had a different tone, perhaps born of desperation brought on by the recent trauma, yet there was also a hunger, a need that matched his own, building upon that flash of connection that had been between them from the first meeting.

"Are you quite certain about this?" he asked when he wasn't claiming her lips.

"Absolutely, I am not, but having this attraction bubble and burn between us is beginning to affect other parts of my life." She tugged at his cravat, and inch by inch, she unraveled the knot and then removed that offending piece of silk along with the collar.

He frowned. "Are you only doing this because you feel vulnerable after what happened to you earlier today?" Then his thoughts scattered as she yanked the buttons from their holes on his jacket. She was so bold and daring, and that stoked his desire and fired his lust.

"I can honestly say I am not." As she spoke, she held his gaze.

"I am not an innocent, Alexander, and neither am I a starry-eyed deb. I'm a grown woman who knows her own mind." Then she wrenched his jacket down his shoulders where it snagged at his elbows. "And in this moment, I know that I want you. Not for a lifetime, not for anything other than two bodies coming together in mutual need and a want for release."

How could he argue with that? It aligned perfectly with what he wished for as well. With a growl, he crushed her into his arms and kissed her soundly while his aroused length pulsed with approval.

Chapter Eight

G OOD LORD, THIS *is truly happening!*

"Then you understand my intent?"

"I'm not a doddering old fool whose faculties have left him, so yes, I do know." There was a decided growl in his voice. He removed his jacket, waistcoat, and shirt with an alacrity that impressed her, them on the floor without a care. "In case you wondered, I want you as well."

"So I discerned from listening to your conversation with your brother yesterday in the salon office." Heat went into her cheeks. "When you spoke about getting beneath my skirts."

"Ah." He shrugged. "It wasn't a lie."

The sight of his bare chest with its light mat of brown hair called to her in a siren song. Unable to stop herself, she ran her palms up his torso, and the rasp of that hair against her skin was heavenly. *Goodness, but I want to spill champagne on him and lick it off.* When she encountered a signet ring hanging on a thin leather chord around his neck that she hadn't seen before, she frowned, touched it with a fingertip, but didn't ask. Now was not the time. "That is good to know. Things go much easier when lying is not part of that foundation."

"Foundation for what?"

It was her turn to shrug. "We shall find out together if your performance tonight impresses me."

"You are quite the minx." His whisper skated over her nape, for he turned her about so that her back was to his chest, then he wrapped his arms around her.

Heated tingles were left in his wake as Alexander trailed his lips over her shoulder to the column of her neck. "I've never met a woman quite like you." When his thumb glanced over the gold, oval-shaped locket she wore, she trembled.

But he didn't mention it. Perhaps he was waiting until after they weren't engaged in foreplay.

"I'm not for everyone, I can assure you, but I refuse to sit back and let life happen to me… or not." A gasp left her throat when he took her breasts in his hands, holding them, squeezing them, teasing the nipples through the fabric of her gown until she whimpered with anticipation.

"Desperate, are you?" he asked, as she arched her back.

"So much," she managed to gasp as he slipped his hands into the bodice of her dress to further stimulate those sensitive peaks. "I crave your hands on me, need to feel your body against mine." If that made her a wanton, then so be it. It had been so long since she'd been involved with a man in a carnal way. "Touch me, Alexander. Show me how much you want me."

"So little patience, in this as you are in every other aspect of life," he murmured and gave her nipples a quick pinch. When she uttered a sound that was a mix of a gasp and a moan, he chuckled. "I have a feeling this coupling will be like nothing I've experienced before." He withdrew his hand from her, and she immediately missed the warmth he'd brought.

"Let us hope so, for I could do with something remarkable in my life just now." With him, she could say or do what she wished and let her true self shine. He'd never shown judgment or censure. There was something safe about him, something that made her crave his protection, even his approval. If she weren't careful, she'd be drunk on the freedom that could be found in him.

Concentrate on the moment, Lydia, not the man. You don't need one in your life, remember.

"Something more remarkable than the strides you are already making by practicing medicine?" Then he proceeded to work the laces at the back of her gown, kissing and nibbling various places on her neck and shoulders as he did so.

"Yes. I sometimes think I'm losing myself in the pursuit of trying to show society that I've found myself, if that makes sense."

"Oddly, it does, and again, I'm sorry. Men who are the powers-that-be in our world are decidedly useless."

Lydia pointed her gaze briefly to the ceiling that was crowded with dancing shadows from the candle's flickering flame. "While I agree, I refuse to stroke your ego with your flirting or the knowledge that you are better than them." When her dress gaped on her person, he shoved it off her shoulders, down her arms and then finally off her body where it pooled at her feet. She gave into a shiver. How much did she adore this part of carnal relations with a man, when passion had nearly taken over?

"Then you have my permission to stroke something else instead," he whispered into her ear and followed the quip with a light nip to her lobe. Once more he caressed and manipulated her breasts, and soon enough, he'd removed her petticoat, stays, and shift. When she stood naked before him except for slippers and embroidered stockings, he groaned. "You are quite a temptation."

"Good, now make good on that."

"I intend to." He maneuvered her away from their shed clothing and guided her over the floor until a wall at her back halted her movement. A curio cabinet and a shelf flanked her on either side. "You are quite fascinating, Miss Tetford, and that is beyond alluring for me." Once he'd urged her arms above her head, he caught her wrists in one hand and cupped a breast with the other.

"Well, I do enjoy being different." She expelled a soft moan when he teased her nipple with his tongue and teeth. "I need you inside me."

"We will eventually arrive at that, but there's nothing stopping you from taking what you want. You are quite a determined woman." With a wink, he released her wrists and then spread his arms wide. "Convince me of your *great* need."

Oh, he was too smug at times. "Don't be an arse more than you can help." If he wanted to play, she would show him exactly why she adored guiding her own life. Lydia dropped to her knees before him and reached for the buttons of his breeches. "Since you *did* ask…" Before he could protest, she'd opened his front falls and then eased his impressively aroused shaft from the fabric. "If you can last more than a few passes, you can choose the position we'll enjoy for coupling."

The breath hissed from him the first moment she touched her tongue to the head of his member. "Have you always been so wicked and troublesome?"

"Yes, because I refuse to accept the status quo." Lydia smiled and then applied herself to her task. She teased the skin just beneath the tip of his gloriously hard, thick shaft, and when she was done, she licked the heated silky skin. Then she took as much of his length into her mouth and throat as she could.

"Oh, God." Alexander held her head in his hands, and the longer she bobbed on his rigid appendage, the more he matched her movements. He thrust into her mouth, his eyes closed, with his head thrown back, his breathing ragged. "You are quite… skilled," he managed to choke out.

"Mmm." Lydia hummed her approval. She fondled his stones as she worked. He'd lasted longer than she'd thought, damn his eyes. Even in this, she had so much freedom, she was giddy from it.

Did the man make the difference?

"Enough." Desperation propelled the word from his throat. Alexander pulled away only to lift her upward to her feet. "Your teasing has brought me too close to the edge."

"That is the point, but show me how much you want me," she demanded, her voice low and throaty with desire. "Take me,

Alexander. Make me forget Colin and his boorish behavior, the fear he imparted."

"Gladly." He pinned her between his hard chest and the wall at her back, and the kisses he treated her to were deep and drugging; he dueled with her tongue as they both fought for dominance, but eventually he won, and she gave herself over to his mastery.

There were times when she wanted nothing more than to lean on someone's strength, and he'd offered that to her, seemingly since the first. It was rather surprising.

When he encouraged one of her legs up, she hooked it over his hip and wrapped her arms about his broad shoulders. His hazel eyes were dark with need; his hands at her buttocks holding her against the wall imparted a thrill. Lydia murmured words of encouragement to him as she wriggled into a better position while anticipation fluttered through her lower belly. She shuddered as he fit his tip to her opening, for she knew he would fill her nicely.

"Why are you delaying?"

"To tease you, of course."

"Rogue." Her moan of satisfaction sounded overly loud to her ears when he flexed his hips and speared into her without stopping until he'd penetrated her to the hilt. Oh, yes, that girth provided wonderfully exquisite sensation. "Mmm, yes." She dug her nails into his shoulders as her eyes shuttered closed. The most delicious feelings bounced through her insides. "So far, you haven't been a disappointment."

"Ah, encouraging." Then he moved, thrusting with short, forceful pushes that set her blood on fire and each nerve ending tingling.

As best as she could, Lydia matched his rhythm, but the position was awkward, and she wanted the release more than she wished to prolong the coupling. Perhaps there would be other times to experience longer couplings. Instead, she hung onto his shoulders and pulled him closer to her body with her leg at his waist.

Over and over Alexander stroked inside her and she clung to him, kissing whatever portion of his body she encountered. The scrape of her sensitive nipples against his heaving chest added another layer to the pleasure she'd already found, as did the friction put on the button at the center of her pleasure, for her body was opened to him and left nothing uncovered. His ragged breathing echoed in her ears. Sweat slicked his back and shoulders. The pungent scent of him filled her nose.

And she couldn't have enough of him.

What is happening to me?

When he delved a hand between their bodies and he strummed his fingers over that swollen bud, a half-stifled scream left her throat. All too soon, the pressure building and circling in her lower belly broke, for the sensory overload had finally overwhelmed her. It was so easy to fall over that edge of bliss with him, and that gave her pause.

Contractions fluttered through her core as pleasure swamped her in ever-increasing waves. She said his name as if in prayer, buried her face in the crook of his shoulder, and still the bands of release kept coming.

Good heavens, he wasn't joking about his skill.

Another two thrusts sent him into the vortex with her. Alexander claimed her mouth in a hard kiss that swept her away. As he ground his pelvis into hers, he lifted her up and she locked her legs around his waist. Completely spent, she collapsed against him, and he did the same to her until they were more or less draped along the wall.

Lydia gave him a tired smile. A pleasant lethargy weighted her limbs. As her heartbeat returned to normal, she sighed and rested a cheek on his shoulder. "Congratulations, Lord Wexley, you have managed to impress me," she whispered in a tired tone.

"Ha!" His chuckle warmed her insides and set off another round of flutters. "I'm glad to know I'm above passing." After several more minutes, he set her onto her feet. "You were amazing—what we shared was incredible."

"Agreed." When she caressed a hand along his chest, touched a fingertip to the signet ring on the thin bit of leather, he uttered a low groan and put a hand over hers, stilling her movement. "I can't take any more just now, but if you allow me an hour's rest, I wouldn't mind going another round with you." There was no mistaking the teasing and need in his voice.

"Ooh, now that *does* sound exciting." And she had completely relegated Colin and his threats to the back of her mind, for now she was firmly committed to pursuing Alexander... within the bounds of having her carnal needs met, that was.

"I have a feeling you can easily become an addiction." The viscount released her, grinning when she teetered on wobbly legs, but he said nothing as they both began the task of dressing.

When she presented him with her back, he tied the laces of her dress, and she did the same for his waistcoat. A sigh sailed from her throat, for it was surely a crime to have his beautiful body covered by clothing. "Do you fancy some tepid tea?"

"That would be lovely. Thank you." As he struggled into his superfine jacket, he came toward the low sofa where she'd settled. "That little session took as much out of me as if I were in the ring."

"Comparing coupling with me to boxing? That's high praise indeed." As she poured out two cups of the amber liquid that was well on its way to being cold, Lydia couldn't help but grin. "And quite the compliment."

"I wouldn't lie about something like this." After Alexander attached his collar, then configured his cravat into some semblance of normalcy, he sat on the sofa beside her. "When is your father expected home?"

"Probably not until midnight." She offered him a teacup, and when their fingers brushed, heated tingles moved up her arm to the elbow. How curious, for she'd assumed once they finally came together, she would cease to have such a reaction to him. "It is good for him to socialize, for he doesn't often have the time for that, and when the fall term begins at Cambridge, he'll be away from London during the week."

"Which means you'll be left alone."

"Perhaps." After downing half the contents in her teacup, Lydia sighed. "I'll look in on his patients as well as help my brother when I can."

"And the other times?"

She shrugged. "I wouldn't mind filling it with boxing lessons." And perhaps she could show him a few jujitsu moves he could incorporate in his routine. "Or other things."

"Ah. I think we can meet those needs—all of them." With a wink, he finished his tea and reached for the teapot. "I assume you've had romantic attachments in the past, if we don't count that bounder, Colin?"

"Yes, he certainly wasn't a romance. A young woman's infatuation, perhaps, and a misguided engagement to please my parents, but not a romance." To her mind, such a state meant being aligned with a man in all the ways that mattered. "Though I took a few lovers over the years, none of those produced romance." Was it wrong of her to mention that part of her history? Perhaps, but she didn't believe in not being truthful. Since they'd already come together carnally, he would have known she wasn't an innocent, even if she hadn't told him prior to that. And she wasn't ashamed of anything she'd done in the past. "Though, where my father is concerned, none of that happened," she said with a grin.

"It is a father's duty to be overly protective of a daughter." Alexander drank from his refreshed cup. "But if I were your brother, I would investigate every man you'd been with to prevent men like Colin from happening."

A queer little flutter moved through her heart from his defense. "I appreciate that, but I can look after myself."

"There is no doubt that you can, but you shouldn't have to. Frankly, I'll feel more at ease if you spend your free time either at the boxing salon or in my company."

"I see." She couldn't help her frown. "I don't appreciate high-handedness from anyone, men in particular. If you think you have a right to possession merely because we coupled—"

"I do not, and that isn't what I meant," he was quick to interrupt with the shake of his head. "I only meant that it would be better if you had people around who will make Colin think twice before attacking you again. Even you, as smart and capable as you are, must see this is a good idea."

"I'll grant you that." There were times when she conceded that being so independent might prove a hinderance to navigating society. Then she sighed. "I'm sorry. You're only trying to help, and I need to learn how to let people who mean well close. To accept assistance." And truth be known, it was rather lovely knowing he wished to look after her.

Alexander nodded. "Good. We all would do well to form friendships." After he finished his tea, he set the cup and the saucer on the table. "Would you like to learn of my romantic entanglements?"

"Only if you wish to tell the stories." When knots of worry formed in her belly, she rested her cup and saucer on the table as well. "Men aren't usually known for opening up about said things."

"Some men, yes. Lewis, for example, struggles with showing emotion or accepting help, just like a certain red-haired woman I've recently met," he said with a sly glance at her.

Heat went through her cheeks. "Not well done of you, Lord Wexley." Then she distracted herself by plucking the remaining pins from her disheveled hair.

A chuckle left his throat to resonate within her chest. "Though there have been a handful of women who have been in my life or graced my bed, I have never been in love with any of them." He grinned. "Unless you count the time when I was a youth of seventeen and went tip over tail for one of my mother's friends. She was a recent widow and a young, attractive one at that." Another laugh escaped him. "Oh, I thought I loved her to the depths of my being. Couldn't eat or sleep. Wanted nothing more from my life than to run away with her, but clearly, it was like a puppy's affection."

What a charming story. "How did you grow past it?"

He shrugged. "Besides having my father pummel some sense into me under the guise of boxing lessons?" When he grinned, she focused her attention on his mouth while plaiting her hair. "Those feelings went away as they usually do, especially after Lewis had a talk with me one day when we were at Papa's country estate. We snuck out after dark one night and into the village. After we went into one of the taverns, he paid a woman to take me upstairs and—"

"Oh, dear." Lydia couldn't help but laugh in delight. "Your brother bought a doxy on your behalf to teach you how to take care of those… urges so you wouldn't continue to lust after your mother's friends."

"Yes." A dark red flush went up his neck and into his cheeks. "After that, things did get easier. That isn't to say I didn't continue to chase women, I just knew how to take the edge off with my hand."

They shared a laugh.

"You sound much like my brother, and I must say, even in that sort of education, it is easier for boys than it is for girls. We are expected to remain pristine and untouched, to never have those thoughts or wonder about what happens between men and women." She shook her head. "Ridiculous, really, when everyone has needs regardless of their gender."

"Agreed, and I must say, your candor and viewpoints are rather refreshing." Then he sobered. "Truth to tell, the women I wished to court as I've gone through my life were more than willing to let me go because I don't command a fortune, and my title is a courtesy from my father and won't be passed down."

"I'm sorry. That must be difficult to know that there are so many shallow women in society who don't value men for themselves." Of course, she knew what such rejection felt like, for even though being a doctor's daughter was slightly more elevated than merely the daughter of a gentleman, without a fortune or a title or wealthy parent, prospects for marriage—if she wanted that—were limited.

"A bit, but since I've trained for bouts, the exercise takes the edge off… mostly." When he met her gaze, he gave her a rueful smile. "Until I meet someone so fascinating I can't ignore her or the desire therein."

A wave of heat went through her body. He was definitely appealing in a sweet but arousing sort of way. "What does the signet ring on the chord mean to you?"

"Ah, I thought you might ask about it." With a finger, he touched the piece of jewelry now hidden beneath his shirt. "It was my father's signet ring. I told Lewis I wanted it after Papa died. I've worn it ever since that horrible day, and it helps me to remember that life is fragile, and that one punch could end everything, so I should enjoy what I can before it's too late." He pressed his lips together before he spoke again. "To be honest, I am terrified of dying in the ring like my father did. Perhaps that is why I'm not as good a boxer as my brothers."

"Wise words and an even better outlook." Perhaps he was more like her than she'd first thought. There was a certain comfort in that. "You are not going to perish in the ring."

"How can you know?"

"Because I refuse to let that happen." As much as she thought boxing for coin was a ridiculous use of one's time, if it was something he enjoyed, then she would attend the bouts. "And I'm going to teach you a few moves of jujitsu that will help you in the ring."

"Thank you." His eyes darkened in the dim light. "I appreciate you not ringing a peal over my head."

"Well, not yet at least," she couldn't help but quip. The soft chime from a carriage-style clock on the shelf indicated the ten o'clock hour. "Will you stay with me for a bit?"

"There is no place I'd rather be." After he scooted backward on the sofa, he brought her with him and tucked her into his side with an arm about her shoulders. "I meant what I said, Lydia, no harm will come to you while I'm around."

She nodded, but instead of using words, she rested a hand on his chest, turned into him, and pressed her lips to his. There was something about this man that spoke to her on a deeper level than she was accustomed to, and frankly, she didn't know how she felt about that.

For the moment, this was enough.

Chapter Nine

August 10, 1817
Stapleton Boxing Salon
Mayfair, London

ALEXANDER WIPED THE sweat from his brow, for the interior of Lewis' office was sweltering with the afternoon sun heating the space even though the blinds were closed and the window glass pushed open.

Unexpectedly, Lydia had arrived in the office from the discreet entrance around the two o'clock hour asking for a lesson. Lewis was out at a private home giving a boxing lesson while Duncan worked the salon floor and could continue to do so himself. He'd been out there with his brother, but when he spied her through the open blinds of the window that looked out into the salon, Alexander had rapidly excused himself, mumbled something about a client in the office, and then beat a hasty retreat there, being certain to close the blinds and prevent any of the other men on the floor from seeing her.

But he'd been ready, for that morning he'd set out a few tick mattresses on the floor as well as had Duncan help him to hang a straw-filled bag in one of the corners of the office. If his brother had questions regarding his behavior, they weren't voiced, and that was fine with him. The less he had to explain or admit to regarding the doctor's daughter, the better.

"Tired already, my lord?" she asked with a sweetly sarcastic note in her voice.

"Perish the thought, Miss Tetford. Merely overheated."

"Then perhaps you should remove your shirt, hmm?" One of her eyebrows went up in challenge, for he'd only stripped to his lawn shirt and breeches.

A shiver of need went down his spine to lodge in his groin when she quite boldly swept her gaze up and down his person as if she wished to devour him whole. And given what she'd treated him to last night, he had no reason to believe she wouldn't.

I rather think I've caught a tigress by the tail.

What would happen if he let go? Half of him wished to find out while the other half did not. "As much as you might beg, the shirt will remain on. We're not finished with the lesson."

She snorted and her chin came up a tiny bit. "You'll *never* hear me beg for anything."

"That's damned disappointing." When he threw a light punch, Lydia blocked it with a mitten-covered hand. "But then, that wasn't what happened last night after we shared tea, was it?" It might make him a rogue to mention that, but part of sparring was trying to distract his opponent, and he grinned. Last night, after the interlude with the tea and enjoying the silence together on the sofa, they'd got up to kissing once more, and that had ended with him sliding off the sofa, pushing up her skirting, and then pleasuring the hell out of her with his fingers, tongue, and lips until she'd hit release twice.

Following that, he'd left the house an hour after that, for he hadn't wished to be in residence when her father returned home, but he'd made her promise she'd come by the salon on the morrow for a boxing lesson.

Pink stained her cheeks. She drilled a fist into his, and the force from that sent him stumbling back a step. "A gentleman wouldn't have mentioned that."

"I never claimed I was a gentleman." Giving her a wink, he swung out a fist and caught her shoulder. The padded mitten prevented him from doing much damage.

"Urgh!" With the shake of her head, Lydia went after him, but he took refuge behind the punching bag. "Why are you so annoying?"

"It must be the company I keep," he said with a wink and a grin. "Now, punch the bag and pretend it's my face."

Her kissable lips pulled downward into a frown. "I don't wish to cause you harm or pain. That is not what a physician does."

"But today, you are not a physician. You are a boxer. Now punch the damned bag. Address everything that makes you fret."

"All right." As he held the bag steady, Lydia gave it a half-hearted punch that barely made a dent in the fabric.

"You can do better than that, my dear."

"I'm not sure…"

"What if I said that a woman should spend her time working on needlepoint and painting, even after she marries, for that is all they're good for?"

"Then I'd come after you with fury." And she did, delivering a one-two punch to the bag with such force behind it that the bag smacked into his chest and cheek.

"Keep going." Pride for her welled in his chest. "Women should only speak when directly addressed."

"You are trodding dangerous ground, Lord Wexley."

Punch, punch!

Her fists slammed into the bag with deadly accuracy.

He couldn't contain his glee, and he laughed. "Quite frankly, I don't believe a woman's mind is capable of reading complex books let alone navigating their way around the human form."

"Argh!" She flew at the bag with her mitten-covered fists drilling into the straw-filled bag. Again and again, she punched that bag until he thought she'd tear through the burlap. "I think I hate you, Alexander."

"Oh, I rather doubt that. You only despise the words you're hearing because countless men have told you those things throughout the course of your life." He came out from behind the bag. "I said them to you to fuel your inner fire, to make you mad enough to use your strength, your inner power, and channel it through your fists."

"While I understand what you're trying to do, it makes me quite mad." With an anguished cry, she came at him, lunging and reaching with her fists, pushing him over the floor toward the tick mattresses. Finally, she caught him, and instead of punching him, she grabbed his right arm with both her hands regardless of the mittens, then she bent her knees, and with another cry, she dropped her hips, pulled on his arm, and before he knew it, Alexander landed flat on his back, staring at her with more than a bit of awe. "And that is but one move I know in jujitsu."

His grin widened as an odd sensation of falling assailed him. "I'm impressed, Lydia. It's too damned bad women aren't allowed to box, because you show real promise."

In a surprise move, she dropped down on top of him, straddling his waist with her skirting hiked up to her thighs. "Do not ever tell me what I can or cannot do, even as motivation." She punched his chest with her mittened hands, but pain shadowed her eyes. "I know what I'm capable of, and I won't be told no just because society deems women should only fit into one mold."

"I would never dream of holding you back or assume to dictate anything to you." Gently, he took her hands in his. "Never have I met such a strong, determined woman of integrity such as you." When he tugged, she came willingly over his chest until her face was mere inches from him. The warmth of her breath skated over his cheek, and damn, the scent of lavender would forever remind him of her. "Truth be told, each time I see you, I'm inspired to do better in my own life, both boxing and personal. You hold yourself to a high standard; there is no reason I can't do the same."

With her as his motivation there was nothing he couldn't do; he fully believed that. Now he understood a bit more of why Lewis had changed so much in such a short period of time. It was for a woman, and perhaps there was a certain comfort in that catalyst.

Her expression softened, and though she smiled, her chin trembled. "I don't know what to say about that, for it's very sweet, but I feel it's also extremely honest. Not many men would dare to show themselves as that vulnerable." Before he could respond, she planted her hands on the tick mattress on either side of his head, layered her upper body against his, and kissed his mouth as if they were alone and the scandal of being imminently discovered wasn't there.

After several moments of indulging her, he eased Lydia off his body and quickly stood, moving behind the punching bag once more to hide his insistent erection, but to her, he hoped it seemed as if he were checking on how the straw interior had shifted. "Too much more of that and you'll find yourself bent over the desk with your skirts over your head."

"As if that is such a bad thing?"

How the hell was he to survive the storm that she represented? For he was confident that she was just that, a storm that blew into his life and then after the destruction, she'd be gone just as quickly. Did he want that, and if he didn't, how to convince her to chase something long term?

"Well, it's not, obviously, but I won't give into base instincts while the salon is full of men having lessons or using the equipment. And not especially if my brothers can come in at any time." He came toward her. "I'm quite selfish, you see, and I want to be the only one to hear your sounds of enjoyment or see your body."

Would that make him seem like a cad?

"Oh." Though a blush stained her cheeks, she offered him a smile. In uncharacteristic silence, she offered her hands. Quickly, Alexander undid the laces and then slipped the mittens from her hands. "Should I remind you that I belong to no one?"

"You can, and while I understand that all too well, I would hope that at least you would give me latitude enough to try and earn your fidelity."

After peering at him for what felt like an eternity, she nodded.

"Should we, uh, continue with the lesson then?"

His nerves suddenly prickled. "I think we've done enough for today, so instead of continuing, what would you say to me escorting you about Town?" Was that too bold?

"Why?" She peered at him with wariness in her expression.

Why indeed. "I… Uh, I am thinking of paying my addresses to you, if you are of the same mind." It was difficult to tell when it came to her.

Lydia propped her hands on her hips. "You? A bachelor with little to no responsibility, and from your own admission not enough coin to set up housekeeping?"

From anyone else, that would have been akin to a slap in the face, but from Lydia, it was an honest barb from a woman who had a penchant for plain speaking. Made a tad better couched in her faint Scottish burr. However, as if a handbell had rung, he had the distinct feeling that he was entering the ring for a new round, and it had nothing to do with boxing, but it was exhilarating just the same.

WAS HE QUITE mad?

Unable to do much more than stare at him in shock, Lydia frowned. "I was just beginning to enjoy what we have recently discovered between us, so why would you wish to ruin that with talk of courtship?" Yet if she were honest with herself, it was flattering to know that an earl's son was interested in her enough to even utter those words.

Even if it unleashed an imp of panic within her chest.

A spark of determination lit his hazel eyes, and drat if his hair, even disheveled, was even more attractive. How the devil did he encourage it to flop over like that? "I rather think it's respecting you instead of treating you on the same level as a courtesan. Meeting clandestinely merely to couple is a bit rude." There was a note of annoyance in his voice, and she couldn't fault him for it. "I think more of you than that."

That took a bit of the wind out of her ire. Clearly, he was a different sort of man than Colin was. "You do?"

"Of course. I mean, God, how wonderous your mind must be to be able to study medicine and prove your intelligence enough that you passed exams many men can't even tackle." The annoyance had changed into awe and the same reflected in his eyes. "I can't begin to fathom memorizing the names of every bone in the human body let alone where each organ is located."

Could he be any more endearing? Her heart squeezed, but this time it wasn't prompted by fear. "While I appreciate that, I'd rather you not enter into a courtship with me if I can't guarantee you what you wish at the end." It would shatter her if she were to inadvertently hurt him when she had no intention of leading him on.

He shrugged. "I'm a patient man, Lydia. And like you, I am quite determined in my own way."

A shiver of need went down her spine, for that confidence was attractive. "But—"

Yet he continued despite her budding objection. "There is no set time for a courtship. It can be a month like what Lewis enjoyed, or it can continue over the course of years until I can order my life, and you can be certain I won't order an end to your ambitions." Step by step, he prowled toward her over the hardwood floor.

"I…" Damn his eyes! He had presented a logical proposition. She retreated until the desk prevented further movement. Despite the fact he was fully offering to do this at a pace she would dictate, fear twisted through her insides, for at the end, regardless of when that was, he would no doubt want marriage. Would she? But his willingness to do whatever she wished as well as protect her from Colin humbled her and left her a bit breathless with wonder. "Oh, Alexander, what am I to do with you?"

"Does that mean we've come to an agreement?" One of his

brown eyebrows lifted as he came into her personal space and slipped his arms around her waist. "You must know there is a connection between us."

"Yes, I have felt it, of course."

"Good, and in order for me—us—to pursue that without scandal breathing down our necks, there should be at least the shell of protection in the guise of a courtship. It is not as binding as an engagement, but it does put other men on notice that I have an interest in you. Additionally, it will appease both your father and my mother. That swath of peace is much needed on both our parts, I suspect."

Why did it make sense? Her heartbeat accelerated. Sweat trickled down her back, pasting her shift to her skin. Would she be signing away her freedom if she did this? Yet he was so compelling, and he intrigued her, for he wasn't like any of the other men she'd met. Everything he did screamed honor and respect, even when she was more critical of him than she should be. Additionally, his touch inflamed her, made her want to continue the path she currently walked. Yet what if she did indeed fall for him? Would that ruin everything she'd worked so hard for? Many men were skilled in lying until they got their way.

"I can almost hear your mind working," he said in a soft voice. "None of the fears you are coming up with will happen. You have my promise."

How did he know her so well already? "And you won't honorably demand we wed merely because we succumbed to passion last night out of some misplaced sense of obligation?"

"Do you want me to? For if something comes from our joining..."

"Do stop." She held up a hand, palm outward. "I just finished my menses; there is no danger of conceiving a child just now."

He nodded. "If there was, I won't leave you in scandal or with a ruined reputation." Then his Adam's apple bobbed with a hard swallow. "In fact, should we come together like that again, I will take measures to prevent such a possibility. You shouldn't be forced into being a mother merely to indulge in a tryst."

And again, he'd impressed upon her how different he was from other men. Oddly enough, tears once more gathered in her eyes. With a sigh, she nodded. "I suppose we have an agreement. With the caveat that I decide when this ends, regardless of the reason."

I need the guaranteed escape.

"I take no issue with that." Then he slid his hands up her sides to eventually hold her head between his palms. "This won't trap you, Lydia, and I certainly promise not to hurt you. In no way do I want to prevent you from meeting any of your dreams; I merely wish to help you do all of that while considering the possibilities. We can support and encourage each other." Then he brushed his lips over her in such a tender kiss that more tears welled until two fat drops fell to her cheeks.

"Why must you be so dratted charming and agreeable?" For the first time in her life, Lydia wanted to melt into a man's arms and let him take up her burdens for a bit while she rested. It was deuced difficult carrying the load and moving against the stream as it were. She brushed at the moisture on her cheeks.

"Perhaps I'm merely fortunate." He waggled his eyebrows, and she couldn't help but laugh. "I'm just glad you met me first before Duncan. Otherwise, you'd be off having adventures with him, for he *is* the more charming of us."

"Oh? Is he a bachelor on the prowl, then?" With a raised eyebrow, she made to move around Alexander. "I do fancy an adventure or two."

"Maddening woman." He tugged her into his arms and kissed her with more conviction. "If adventure is what you want, that is what I'll give you."

The poor man came up to the mark quite splendidly. She patted his cheek. "The only adventure I want is perhaps being driven along Rotten Row. If you truly wish for a courtship, then by all means let us be seen in the most popular place in Mayfair together."

"You want a drive?" Surprise lined his face, quickly followed by a trace of disappointment. "That's all?"

"For the moment." She winked. "You do have a carriage, don't you?" The sad fact was, if he hadn't sorted himself and didn't have the requisite coin to even keep a carriage, there wasn't much hope for the future—together for legitimate purposes or even for him to ask her to become his mistress.

I know my worth and I won't come cheap.

"Of course I do." As he pulled away, she caught a hint of concern in his eyes. "I'll merely borrow Lewis' open carriage. I'm sure he's not using it. In fact, I'll go outside and find an urchin, pay him to deliver a missive to the mews."

Lydia nodded. "I need to don my bonnet and gloves, but I will meet you on the pavement in a bit." Once he'd gathered his hat and gloves, Alexander left the office, and with a sigh, she sat on the chair behind the desk. What had just happened?

Surely this tingly feeling will go away. It's just the excitement of knowing the tryst isn't quite over. Isn't it?

Chapter Ten

August 12, 1817

Alexander groused as he strolled the walking paths in Hyde Park with Lydia at his side. He hadn't seen her for two days due to their respective commitments and schedules, but now he regretted asking her to go for a ride with him, for they'd once more taken Lewis' open carriage and now as they were deep in the park, a steady rain had started. A quick glance upward through the trees showed the overcast skies wouldn't clear.

"Perhaps I should escort you back home, for we will both be drenched soon."

She squeezed her fingers on his arm. "There are worse things, Lord Wexley. Being drenched does have its advantages if you think about it," she said in a low, throaty voice that went straight to his stones.

Heat filled his chest. "Do you always do and say scandalous things, or has meeting me brought it out in you?"

A trill of laughter escaped her, and he rather liked the dulcet sound. "Isn't my being female and practicing medicine scandal unto itself?"

"To be honest, if I'm in a bad state that requires a physician, it doesn't matter to me who attends to my wounds." The prevailing idea that a woman didn't have the intelligence to do such a thing boggled his own mind. From what he'd seen of women recently—though his experience was somewhat limited—women were fully capable of doing fantastic things, but they only needed the chance to shine.

"I would like to hope that sentiment would transfer to society at large, but I fear we are years, perhaps decades, away from that." She patted his arm. "As for the rain, well, when does London not have a week without rain?" When she turned her head and met his gaze, humor lurked in the green depths of her eyes. "We won't die from a few raindrops."

As she spoke, the rain came down even harder, which prompted a laugh from them both.

"Well, since we're so deep in the park and far from where my driver is waiting, we should probably find some sort of shelter," Alexander mentioned as he hustled her along the pathway. "If the rain lets up, we'll make our way back to the entrance arch."

"There are worse people to spend the time with." Then she left his side, and before he could question why, Lydia darted into a clearing, spread her arms wide, and twirled about with her face lifted to the sky.

In that moment, when her tinkling laugh tripped through the air and the joy on her face had the power to light the dreary overcast gloom, he lost a tiny piece of his heart to her. Unexpected, that, but there was nothing he could do about it. Seeing her twirl about despite the heavy rain without seemingly a care for the state of her clothing, her bonnet which had fallen backward to hang around her neck by its ribbons, or how society might judge her once they made their way back, he was suddenly envious of that unique kind of freedom.

"Come, Alexander, join me!"

Oh, what the hell? Where was the harm? Tossing his cares to the proverbial wind, he met her in the clearing, where she immediately took his gloved hands and urged him into an impromptu dance. Rain fell on his face. It drummed on his top hat and quickly seeped through his jacket of sapphire superfine. But there was something about cavorting about with this woman that allowed his soul to soar for a bit.

Only when he was completely soaked, and Lydia's skirts were stuck to her lower limbs did he bring them to a halt. "You are quite unexpected," he mentioned in a soft voice as he reeled her into his arms.

"That is a good thing, because why would anyone want dull and expected?"

"Indeed." Then he kissed her because he could. There was something free and easy about tasting her lips that were dotted with raindrops. So far, the tentative dip into this courtship had been as unorthodox as their first meeting, but then he wasn't a Stapleton for nothing. And frankly, standing in the rain with their clothing plastered to their bodies, basically alone in the world just now was one of the most memorable moments in his life to date. When he pulled away, he grinned like an idiot. "Let's find shelter. Playing in the rain is fine for a time, but I don't wish to camp out in it."

"Perhaps you're right. Already, this dress is uncomfortable."

Nestled within the trees at the end of the footpath was a small stone structure that had a bit of a roof. Built to resemble an old Roman temple, it was no doubt a folly for decoration or to perhaps allow people on foot a rest before walking back to the opposite side of the park or toward the Serpentine, but it would serve their purposes nicely.

"At least this will keep the rain off us for a while," he said as he pulled her into the open-air structure. A crumbling marble bench rested in the middle of the marble floor, and he showed her onto it while he chose to remain standing. "I can't remember the last time I actually had fun in the rain, so thank you for that."

"Well, just remember why you wear your father's signet ring. Life is short, Alexander." She held his gaze. "We shouldn't go through it all clouds and grumble just because things aren't going the way we want."

"Now who is the one offering wise words?" In this way, she kept him grounded, and he needed that, perhaps now more than ever. With a sigh, he shoved his hands through his hair, leaving it in wet, furrowed rows. "If you have any insight for me regarding boxing, I wouldn't mind hearing it."

Lydia frowned. "Meaning what? Are you planning to retire from the sport? I thought you enjoyed it."

"I do, but we both know I'm not a champion like my brothers or even my father, and I do need the coin winning bouts bring, but I suspect that I need to start thinking logically about my future." As he regarded her, his chest tightened. "What will I do if I'm not actively boxing? It is my father's legacy." Was it something he was willing to walk away from?

She paused in the act of pulling her wet skirting away from her legs. "Do you enjoy doing anything that has nothing to do with boxing? Or do you have skills and talents in a different area?"

"Well, I can't sing or play an instrument or perform, if that's what you're asking." A chuckle left his throat. "And I suppose seeing me from your eyes, I'm quite useless as an earl's son. Isn't that what you've told me?" When a blush sprang into her cheeks, he shrugged. "It's all right. For many years, I have been a bit reckless, though Duncan holds the title for that. And I suppose I *am* a useless bachelor, for at the age of one and thirty, I haven't made inroads into being anything other than that and a boxer."

God, I'm making it worse.

For long moments, Lydia regarded him with speculation in her expression. Then she plucked the pins from her hair, setting each one on the bench beside her. "When you wake in the morning, what is the first thing you immediately think of?"

"I…" When he truly ruminated on it, he sighed. "Boxing. I sometimes dream about each new technique I've learned, how I can move my feet faster, what I need to do in order to win."

"Yet, from your own admission, you aren't as skilled in it as your brothers." It wasn't a question.

"That is correct." He shrugged.

"If you were to ask me the same question, my answer would be tending to patients, setting them at ease, helping them heal whatever is wrong." She shook out her wet hair, ran her fingers through the fiery waterfall, and damn if she didn't resemble a Scottish witch in that moment, surrounded by the wooded area, holding court in the marble structure. "You and I, Alexander, we are creatures of deep purpose. We know where we should be in this life and why. What's more, we won't let circumstances or anyone stop us from reaching those goals."

"That doesn't answer my question though." It was fascinating to watch her plait her hair, and once the tresses were secured, she wound the length around the back of her head and secured it with the pins in a tidier look than she'd had before.

"I honestly don't believe you can remove boxing from your life and continue to be happy."

He nodded. "That is true, but I detest doing the salon's books, which is where my brother seems to think I belong. If given half a chance, I'd be a good manager, but Lewis is controlling."

"Then continue to work on him. Put a plan together of what you would like to accomplish or see happen if you should be given free reign over the salon. Appeal to his logical side regarding the business. Outline for him how a streamlined salon would turn a greater profit." She shrugged. "What have you got to lose?"

How much did he appreciate her insight and seeing the problem from a different view? "You make me feel as if there is hope."

"There is always that, Wexley." Then she pulled a small, brass hand mirror from the reticule that matched the blue and ivory striped dress. "Speaking of the salon, you need something that might set it apart from the others in Mayfair."

"Such as?"

After checking her face in the looking glass, Lydia replaced it into the bag. "Consider that it might be a good thing to have a doctor attached to the salon, to attend to the injuries that naturally occur there, or at the very least, to manage your clients' vital signs."

His eyebrows rose. "Meaning?" Excitement buzzed at the

base of his spine, for he had an inkling that she was unconsciously trying to find ways to keep them together or aligned. Was she aware of that, or was this how she could justify a courtship in her own mind?

"Just this." Mirth twinkled in her green eyes. "The other day I saw a space in the neighboring building for let. It would be ideal to set up a clinic or a discreet physician's office there."

"Indeed." He rubbed a hand along his jaw. "For your own purposes connected with the boxing salon or to move your father's patients to the new location?"

"I haven't decided since the idea has only recently taken root." She shrugged and again pulled at her wet skirting. "Before I do anything, I will need to talk to my father, for I'll need his assistance with the real estate."

"It would be a delight to have you so close." Which meant that he would need to stay at the salon in some fashion.

"That's what I was thinking too." Briefly, she bit her bottom lip as she looked up at him. "You wouldn't mind, would you?"

"Not at all, though the temptation to fall into scandal will be high." Unless they were to marry… He shook his head. *Don't rush your fences, Wexley. She's far too skittish about that.*

"What is life without something to look forward to?" When she stood up from the bench, she shook out her skirting as best she could, but it was apparently a hopeless cause to keep the wet fabric from sticking to her legs. "I think my father will be pleased."

"How can you know that?" He didn't offer a protest when she put her palms on his chest and drew them upward to rest her wrists on his shoulders.

"I prefer to take a hopeful approach because I know the goals I wish to reach."

"Hmm." His gaze dropped to her mouth. "Am I one of them?"

"We shall see." Then she raised onto her toes and fit her lips to his.

Several moments went by as they exchanged gentle kisses, and within that embrace, he had a few glimpses of an amazing future that might prove his if he was as patient as he'd told her he was a couple of days ago.

Eventually, Alexander pulled away. "Have you ever considered not being a doctor or becoming a physician?"

"Absolutely not. I knew that from a young age, and quite honestly, I won't stop until that is what I am." Nothing but truth reflected in her eyes. "I'll tell you this, also. If you aren't part of that plan, if you aren't willing to walk that difficult path beside me, I will need to go ahead by myself, for I have already experienced having a man in my life who is at counterpoint to my vision."

His respect for her continued to rise. "You humble me with your determination, push me to working harder in boxing… or the management of the salon."

"Does that bother you?"

"Oddly enough, it does not." The grin he offered widened. "I think that insistent push is what I've needed all along, especially with Lewis not being present as much as he used to be." Then he really looked at her. "How do you feel about all this?"

"I am… cautiously optimistic, and I know that I'm a managing baggage and quite bossy at times." Worry shadowed her eyes. "While I realize that men don't like women to behave in this way, I can't, in good conscience, act like all the others because I have this passion inside me that tells me not to give up."

"Good Lord, don't change yourself to be more like what society says a woman *should* be, because I will tell you another truth." He put his lips to the shell of her ear. "The best men are not searching for perfect society women. We will go quite happily mad for a woman with spirit and fight in her."

That was something he'd come to believe in himself over the past few years, and perhaps that was one of the reasons why he'd never found just the right one who could prove a helpmeet.

The relief and pleasure in her expression was all the reward he needed for speaking the truth. "The more time I spend with you, the more I'm convinced you are something special indeed, Lord Wexley, and that is quite a feat, for men don't tend to impress me."

"So I have seen." With a laugh, he tugged on her hand and led her from the folly. "We should head back while there is a slight break in the rain."

"I rather hope there is tea waiting for us somewhere, laced heavily with a good Scottish whisky."

What had her childhood been like? He didn't know but was desperate to hear the stories. Perhaps he should make strides to meet her father.

They were halfway into the journey back to the opposite side of the park when a large man stood in the middle of the bridal path with his arms crossed at his chest, standing there with a glare that seemed focused clearly on Lydia.

"Who the devil is that?"

She gasped beside him. "My former fiancé, Colin MacIntosh." Before he could do anything else, Lydia marched up the path to confront the other man. "What are you doing here, Colin? If you think to bully me, I'll need to disabuse you of that notion."

Easily, the big Scot stepped around her in order to close the distance between him and Alexander. "*This* is who ye've replaced me with?"

A snort of annoyance escaped her as she trailed behind him. "That is the Viscount Wexley, so mind your manners."

"Ha! A title doesn't make a man." The bigger fellow shook his head. "He is a scrap of a man and not even Scottish!"

"Nowhere is it written that I need to find myself engaged to a Scot!" Frustration clearly rang in her voice, but Mr. MacIntosh ignored her.

No wonder she broke their engagement.

"Oh, ye'll still marry me, mark my words, but first, I'm going to put *Lord* Wexley in his place and show him he has no right to you."

Alexander glanced at Lydia, who glowered back. "I rather think it's you who have no right to her, Mr. MacIntosh. The lady has already declared that you are unfit by breaking the engagement between the two of you. Now do the honorable thing and leave her be."

"Listen to the viscount, Colin," Lydia said as she laid a staying hand on one of his large arms. "I am not going back with you. It's been over a year. Enough already."

"You don't get to make that decision!" In the process of shaking off her touch, Colin also gave her a shove, and she stumbled off the bridal path.

"You'll pay for that," Alexander said in a low, controlled voice that rumbled with the anger he felt. Without missing a beat, he lunged and threw a punch, catching the other man on the chin.

Unfortunately, Colin only grunted before swinging a meaty paw in retaliation. The fist connected with Alexander's shoulder with enough force that it spun him about.

"You damned oaf." The man needed a lesson. Though Lydia implored him from the side of the path, he flew at the Scotsman in a fury of fists. An uppercut landed in the bigger man's temple and while he worked through the disorientation, he jabbed a fist into Colin's breadbasket, which winded him. "Stay away from her, Mr. MacIntosh. Miss Tetford has soundly rejected you."

That apparently enraged the other man, for Colin came at Alexander with a roar. He wasn't as slow as he appeared, for when the right hook came, Alex wasn't ready for the impact. It caught him on the chin with enough force to crash his teeth together and send him sailing onto his back, where he landed hard on the ground.

"Wexley!" Lydia's cry sounded overly loud in the rain and the hush of the wooded area.

Colin wiped at the sweat on his forehead. "This isn't over between us, my lord." He pointed a thick finger at Alexander. "The woman is mine. When next we meet, I won't stop until you are broken and bleeding." Then, with a rude gesture at Lydia, he loped away. Seconds later, he vanished around the curve of the path.

"Are you hurt?" Lydia asked as she reached his side and fell to her knees. Before he could answer, she rushed onward. "You're an idiot, Alexander." She skimmed her gloved hands over his person, no doubt checking for injuries. "You should have walked away."

"Stop." He captured one of her hands, stilling it as he struggled into a sitting position. The whole of his backside was covered in mud. "I refuse to let him boss you or me. Frankly, Lydia, you are not an object to be owned and are worth more than he thinks. Therefore, I will defend such a treasure." *What a nodcock thing to say, Wexley.* His chest tightened for waxing poetic and perhaps showing too much of his budding feelings. "At least my clock wasn't cleaned. It was only a couple of punches." Yes, they hurt like the devil, but he'd gotten off jabs of his own.

"Oh." As she sucked in a breath, she stared at him with rounded eyes as if seeing him for the first time. "That is so sweet." Unexpectedly, she launched herself into his arms.

"Oomph!" They both tumbled onto the wet, muddy ground to one side of the bridal path. "Lydia!"

"I can't help it," she said in between kissing his lips. "As I said, you have managed to impress me, and you continue to do so. It is quite an aphrodisiac."

Who was he to bid her nay, then?

Some time later, he finally encouraged her off him so that he could gain his feet. "My dear, your skirting is hopelessly stained, and the dress ruined. Such a scandal."

"As if you are walking the straight and narrow, Mr. Muddy Arse?" She flashed a smile. "I don't mind if you don't."

"I do not. In for a penny, in for a pound, heh?" He tugged her back onto the path so they could finally make their way out of the rain. "Well, I am all in, Miss Tetford, so you'd best square with that."

All in all, it had been a successful outing even if he would feel those new bruises like hell on the morrow. But his spirits soared, for it seemed likely the independent thinking doctor's daughter was coming 'round to the idea that a courtship between them would indeed work.

Chapter Eleven

August 14, 1817
Mrs. Cooper's Chocolate House
Mayfair, London

I T HAD BEEN two days since the rainy walk in Hyde Park with Viscount Wexley. Two days since Colin had bedeviled them and tried to take Alexander on in an impromptu fist fight. Two days since she'd felt that odd little lilt and tickle through her heart that heralded other, more troubling symptoms.

Good heavens, please don't let me fall in love with him!

So if that wasn't it, how exactly did she feel for him? She hadn't lied when she'd told him that he'd managed to impress her. In fact, the handsome boxer with the mane of brown hair had managed to sneak around her defenses and set up camp in front of her heart, continually pounding until she let him in.

Ideally, she wished to keep him around to relieve a carnal itch, but he was more than that, out of sheer tenacity. Would he ask her to be his mistress, and if he did, would she go for it? That would allow her to enjoy him, enjoy a physical relationship without the hassle of being married. Yet she suspected he would want to take her to wife, because that was the sort of man he was.

Adorably honorable yet annoying.

Except... over the last few times she'd been together with him, in bed or out, he'd proved time and again he wasn't an objectionable sort. In fact, if she could have picked the exact kind of man she'd want at her side to help meet the lofty goals that she had, someone like Alexander would have fit that bill.

Drat his eyes.

All of that to say that she was becoming far too fond of him, and if things continued in that vein, she'd be ready lock, stock, and barrel to meet him on a marriage altar without complaint like all the other silly women of the *ton* who had nothing else better to do with their futures.

Why is this so difficult to puzzle out?

Which was what led her to the chocolate house. When her mind was conflicted, she always took refuge in sweets, and since there was a chocolate house near her brother's clinic, she stopped inside for a cup of drinking chocolate as well as tea with plenty of pastries.

The viscount was a large conundrum.

No sooner had she settled onto a wrought iron chair at a small, round table near a front window with a warmed porcelain cup full of thick melted chocolate in her hand did she happen to glance out at the foot traffic that came into the cul-de-sac from Brook Street at the other end. Then her heart gave an odd sort of flutter, and tingles went through her lower belly as she spied a familiar form walking along the pavement.

Oh, dear.

It should be criminal for a man to look that splendid. To say nothing of how much a ninny she was gawking at him out the window. What was Alexander doing in this part of Mayfair? Perhaps he had a scheduled appointment, for there were two solicitors in the immediate area, or perhaps he was on his way back from a private boxing lesson. After all, the boxing salon was located at the opposite end of Brook Street. Or perhaps he just merely wished to walk for exercise… since he didn't keep his own carriage. Still, as she sipped the rich chocolate, Lydia continued to stare, and stopped herself short of uttering a sigh of appreciation aloud.

No matter that he sported a few new bruises on his face, he was still the most attractive man she'd laid eyes on in quite a while. With his top hat sitting at the usual rakish angle over his left eye and his thick brown hair dancing in the slight summer breeze, he was far too handsome to be wandering through Mayfair garnering looks from women passing by him on the pavement. A twinge of hot jealousy stabbed through her chest. What if he caught one of them staring and sparks flew between them?

Well, I'm not done with him yet!

Something must be done, of course, if only to protect him from himself. With a knuckle, she rapped on the glass. Once, twice, and finally on the third time, he must have heard it while he'd paused to talk briefly with a male acquaintance. When he turned and glanced into the window, his whole face lit with recognition as he saw her.

Oh, dear. A queer little squeeze went around her heart, for he was beyond endearing. *I'm in a spot of bother, I think.*

As he pantomimed that he would come in and join her, she nodded with a smile, and as confusion filled her, she took refuge in her drinking chocolate again. When the slightly bitter, complex notes of the treat settled on her tongue, her gaze went across the small dining area that hosted perhaps ten tables in total. A few shelves and a curio cabinet set amidst the room housed bric-a-brac figurines and mismatched porcelain teacups and saucers that lent a cozy feeling to the space.

Seconds later, Alexander appeared. He spoke with the owner of the establishment, gestured toward Lydia's table, and then he made his way to her. As he did, more than one woman glanced his way with admiration, and she felt quite smug, because at least for the moment, he was hers.

"Good afternoon, Miss Tetford," he said, and even though he used a low voice, there was something about how he uttered the words that sent tingles of need down her spine. "Thank you for the impromptu invitation." He sat upon a wrought iron chair that matched hers, sent a look across the close confines of the small table that sent heat into her cheeks. "I am glad to see you today."

She nodded but held back a response, for a maid brought the tea service Lydia had ordered to the table. To the young woman, she said, "If you could bring an additional cup and saucer, please? I have an unexpected guest who joined me."

"Of course, mum." Then the maid left, winding her way through the tables.

"Thank you for coming. I have found I have rather missed you since we were caught in the rain." How would the admission affect him? When he said nothing, but an easy grin curved his sensual lips, she smiled back. "How have you been keeping yourself?"

"Busy, of course. Lewis signed a handful of new clients, so we've been working out lesson schedules. Then my mother summoned me for tea yesterday when I would have called upon you. Mama doesn't take no for an answer."

"Did she harangue you over your continuing bachelor state?"

"A bit, though she did hint at the gossip that is apparently circulating through the *beau monde* that says I've signaled out a young woman and have been seen driving her about Mayfair," he said with a wink.

"And who, pray tell, is the fortunate lady?"

The maid returned to the table with the cup and saucer. Alexander nodded his thanks, and when Lydia poured tea into his cup, he said, "I think you know."

Heat seeped into her cheeks. "I do." And that knowledge sent another round of confusion through her mind. Once she'd finished with his cup, she poured a measure of the amber liquid into her own teacup even though she hadn't drunk all the chocolate. "How does your mother feel about that? And does she know that I wish to be a physician?"

Alexander calmly put a small lump of sugar into his cup, then followed it with a splash of cream. As he stirred the brew with a silver teaspoon, he regarded her with shadows in his hazel eyes, so striking with the sun that came in through the window. "While my mother is decently accepting that I've shown an interest in a woman, she is rather less than amused at the fact said woman isn't the demure and typical society type."

"Ah." Her chest tightened from the unexpected secondhand censure. It wasn't the first time she'd been judged, but this time it hurt, and that was a surprise, for she wasn't aware she'd hoped to make a good impression on his mother. "I'm sorry to hear that."

"If things progress further between us, Mama will come around. I wouldn't worry too much about her, for she was vehemently against the lady that Lewis chose as well." One of his eyebrows rose as he held her gaze. "Trust me?"

Did she? Finally, she nodded, took a sip of the chocolate. "It matters not, I suppose. I can only be the woman I'm meant to be, and giving all that up merely to please a potential mother-in-law would be doing myself a grave disservice."

I would rather remain unattached than let go of my dreams.

"I'm not asking you to change, Lydia," he said in a whisper. After a quick glance around, Alexander briefly laid a hand atop hers. "One of the reasons you appeal so strongly to me is your unconventional nature and your lofty dreams."

"Thank you." Her own whisper was a bit choked. What she needed right now was a distraction or else she would tumble into the brown-green pools of his eyes. "Try this." She pushed the cup of drinking chocolate toward him. "Chocolate is my Achilles heel. Whenever my mind is beset with confusion or I am an emotional mess, I turn to something sweet, and usually that treat is chocolate... or the cream inside pastries... or even sometimes champagne."

"Now that is an interesting insight about you." When he lifted the cup to his lips and took a drink, his eyebrows shot up into his hairline. "That is quite something. Thick, sweet yet not overly so, with just enough viscosity that it almost coats the throat when I swallow."

She nodded. "It is exceptional when it's hot. Sometimes I thin it out with milk or even coffee if it is available."

"Oh, coffee would prove amazing in this." He took another drink, then rested the cup on the table. "Is that why you're here this afternoon? Because your mind is conflicted?"

"It is."

"Because of me?"

"Partially. I am also trying to puzzle out where I would like my future to go beyond having you in it." She frowned, dropped her attention to the amber depths of her teacup. "Is it folly to continue to push, to fight so hard for my own place in this world when seemingly everyone is against that?" Knots of worry, or perhaps fear, pulled in her stomach. "As much as I believe fully that I am here to practice medicine, will I miss out on other equally vital parts of life if I pursue this? Am I harming my reputation by continuing to go against societal norms?"

Harming your reputation by keeping company with me?

"I have had those moments. Hell, I'm second guessing myself right now and fighting with the same doubts regarding what I'm supposed to do in my own future, as you know." He paused to take a drink of tea. "However, none of that means you—we—are on the wrong track. It merely means we aren't content to go with the status quo in chasing the life we truly want."

"Why must you always present things in such a logical manner that it helps soothe my nerves?"

He shrugged with a grin as he reached for a honey cake on the tea tray. "Perhaps I just have that knack."

"Mmm." When tears prickled the backs of her eyelids, Lydia blinked until the urge to cry passed. She cleared her throat. "Did you know that chocolate was once used in ancient Aztec cultures as currency as well as an aphrodisiac?"

"I did not." Again, he sent a glance about the immediate area. No one paid the slightest attention to them. He lowered his voice to a barely audible whisper. "However, where you are concerned, I don't need enhancements or things to help stir my desire." When he winked, shivers of the same played her spine. "You alone have my attention, and I'm as addicted as an opium addict."

Dear heavens, he is so charming! "Must be the hair and the faint accent," she said in a breathless whisper. "I have been told I'm quite fascinating."

"Without a doubt you are."

While Alexander happily made a feast of some of the pastries on the tray, she had the odd notion of continuing to tease him. He made it so easy, and he also made her feel quite daring at times. "What if I told you that I wished we were alone with this cup of drinking chocolate because I want nothing more than to lick it from your naked body?"

"Is that right?" A red flush made its way up his neck and into his cheeks as his eyes rounded.

"Oh, yes." She took another sip of the chocolate, and when a drop of it clung to her bottom lip, she whisked it away with the tip of her tongue, making sure that he watched. In the veriest of whispers, she continued. "Can you imagine what that would feel like as I chased a trail of chocolate down your torso, past that wonderfully ridged abdomen, and then finally swirled my tongue around the tip of your oh so rigid member, so I could lick away every bit of that dark sweetness?"

The dear man shifted on his chair. Did that mean he needed to accommodate a burgeoning arousal? "The only way I would allow that would be if I could return the favor." Wicked promise glittered in his eyes as he kept his voice to a bare whisper. "I would make certain to drizzle that liquid brew over your breasts and spend copious amounts of time licking every bit of it away from your soft skin, paying intense attention to your sensitive nipples." When he again touched her hand, Lydia nearly jumped in her chair. "But I wouldn't stop there."

"Oh?"

"I would not. In fact, I would continue to lick that thin trail of chocolate down your body, suck it away from your skin, and during the quest to leave none of the sticky substance behind, I might blow a breath over the wetness. When gooseflesh rippled on your belly, I would continue my path, over your mons, spreading you open as I went, just to make certain none of that lovely chocolate had found its way to that swelling button at your center. Then I would close my lips around that bud, suckle it while flicking it with my tongue."

"Do stop," she implored in a whisper as she fanned her face with a hand.

"Never say you're wildly uncomfortable, Miss Tetford." Humor threaded through his voice. "Perhaps you should go straight home if you're feeling feverish."

"Rogue." She shook her head. He played the game as well as she. "Too bad we're not at a corner table, for I'd try for some stimulation and perhaps slip over the edge either with your help or not." It took all her willpower not to touch that spot between her thighs through her skirting to relieve the ache of longing he'd started with his words. But even she wasn't that daring or bold.

His Adam's apple bobbed with a hard swallow, but his eyes had darkened. "I would be happy to assist you in that, if you would like to remove from this place?"

With a grin, she shook her head. "I would rather finish my tea, but I have no doubt that you might prove my downfall if I'm not careful."

Quickly, his expression sobered. "There is no doubt that I'll be there to catch you if you fall, Miss Tetford."

"So I am beginning to see." She took refuge in sipping her tea. Oddly, the thought didn't incite as much fear as she thought it would.

"Tell me about your locket. I've seen you wear it a few times, and now I'm curious." He gave her another wink. "At least it will give us both a distraction."

"Indeed." She touched a fingertip to the golden oval that rested just above the tops of her breasts. Then she gingerly opened the locket so he could see the tiny painted portraits of her parents. "This is my mother and father shortly after they were married. I adored how they were during that time in their lives, and if I ever marry, I would like to hope my union will be as solid and as full of love and respect as theirs was."

Alexander peered at the miniatures, then he closed the locket with a snap. "You resemble both your parents." Again, he touched her hand. "I'm sorry about the loss of your mother."

"Thank you. I miss her every day. Sometimes, I think to turn to her and tell her something… but she's not there, and the grief hits me anew." Once more, she had no choice except to show vulnerability in front of him. "I wear the locket to keep them both close, and to also remember that love is nothing to sneeze at."

"Or nothing to avoid out of fear?" he added in a low voice.

"Yes." How did he know her so well? "Yet the fear persists, for life is fragile, as you well know. My mother perished from an ailment she should have been able to fight." She pressed her lips together as she thought about her next words. "I am a physician without the credentials, but I am well aware of the dangers that come with pregnancy and childbirth. It is quite terrifying. Perhaps that is also why I'm avoiding being wed." Tears welled in her eyes. "I can't explain it better than that."

"While I understand what you are saying, and I have those same fears—because who wants to lose a wife in the process of birthing a child who might also die?—please try to bear in mind that when you wed, you will not be alone. And if the man you select cares anything about you, if you truly don't wish for children, he will make every effort to follow those wishes."

"Even if it's not fair to him?" she couldn't help but ask.

"Marriage means a partnership, and as far as I'm concerned, that means treating a wife as an equal in everything—including decisions that affect a shared future." He shrugged. "Love is powerful, Lydia, and can be enjoyed no matter what happens between a couple. The key is communication, so don't think to keep your concerns bottled up."

"I'll try and remember that," she managed to gasp out, as a couple of tears fell to her cheeks. It boggled her mind that Alexander was so different in his thinking than Colin. When he gave her his handkerchief, she nodded her thanks, then dabbed at her cheeks. His scent clung to the fabric, and she surreptitiously sniffed it.

"Don't borrow trouble, Miss Tetford," he said in a slightly louder voice, then laid a hand on hers. When she turned her hand palm upward, she threaded their fingers together and clung to him for a few seconds before putting her hands in her lap. "Fate is not done with you yet, and unless I miss my guess, you will not meet misery."

"How can you know that?"

He grinned. "You are too forthright to let that happen."

"Perhaps." Hiding a smile behind her teacup, she stifled a sigh.

What am I to do with you?

Chapter Twelve

August 15, 1817
Stapleton House
Marylebone, Mayfair
London, England

WHEN ALEXANDER ENTERED the drawing room in Stapleton House—his former home until Lewis had married—he stifled a groan to find not only Duncan there but also his mother.

Since Lydia had a prior commitment with her father that evening—she was attending a rout—he'd decided to call on his brother and perhaps ask Lewis' council on the matter of the doctor's daughter.

Yet now there was an audience, and he didn't want or need that.

"Ah, Alexander, how lovely to see you here tonight too," Lewis greeted from his position at the sideboard. Currently, he poured out two cut-crystal glasses of brandy while the new countess talked quietly with the dowager on a low sofa. "Sit, sit. It will be good to have an at-home this evening and to share a meal like we used to."

"Indeed." He crossed the floor, and at the sofa where his mother sat, he leaned over and bussed her cheek. "Good evening, Mama." Afterward, he took Cecilia's hand, brought it to his lips, and kissed the back. "Countess."

Both ladies tittered while Duncan snorted from his position on the sofa opposite theirs.

"Doing it up too brown brother," Duncan said with the shake of his head.

Dropping onto a cushion beside his brother, Alexander peered at him. "There is nothing wrong with showing a bit of charm and class, even if it's only to family. You should practice that sometime."

"Don't think to lecture me in deportment. I'm by far more charming than you." A chuckle came from his brother.

"Stop, the two of you," their mother said with a sniff. "It has been far too long since we were all together as a family."

Alexander snorted. "We were just together for Lewis' nuptial ceremony a month ago, Mama. That's hardly an age." When Lewis brought over glasses of brandy and gave them to both him and Duncan, he grinned. "Thank you."

"You are welcome. I'm glad you came for dinner." Lewis took his own glass to a chair near his mother's location.

"As am I." A meal was a meal, and if he didn't need to pay for it, all the better. Some foods were still scarce due to last year's mess of not having a summer when crops failed, but to be honest, his appetite had been lagging ever since he'd met Lydia. "What is on the menu tonight?"

The new countess smiled. "Roasted chicken in cream sauce for the main. Beyond that, I don't remember, for doing the menus weekly isn't something I especially excel at."

"It will come easier with time, dear," their mother said as she patted Cecilia's hand.

"You are doing an incredible job, Cecilia," Lewis said with enough obvious affection in his gaze as he looked at his wife that Alexander felt a touch uncomfortable.

"Do hush, Lethbridge," she murmured with a blush in her cheeks. "I am trying my best."

Lewis sipped his own brandy with an indulgent smile. "What brought you out here tonight, Alex? Thinking of entering another bout? There's one coming up, but I'm not certain if there are empty spots or not." He shot a glance to Duncan. "Is there?"

Duncan shrugged. "I don't believe so, unless one of the fighters drops out, but if you want me to put Alex's name on the wait list, I will."

Excitement buzzed at the base of Alexander's spine at the prospect of boxing for prize money again. "I'm interested."

Their mother frowned. "Didn't Lewis' injuries last month show you that boxing isn't good for your health? It is a waste of time besides." She shook her head. "I wish you boys wouldn't put yourselves into harm's way with it; I don't care that you consider fighting your father's legacy."

"It is better to claim bare knuckle boxing as a gift from Papa than knowing we all have to scrimp and work a trade to fill the empty coffers." With a shrug, Alexander left the relative safety of the sofa in order to pace the floor in front of the cold fireplace. Since the windows were open, a summer breeze wafted into the room, redolent with the scent of flowers and the smell of the air just before it rained. "I'm not interested in having a discussion about this, Mama. These are the circumstances, and we are all trying to find our way through."

"Is the boxing salon turning a profit, then?" his mother wanted to know. On the surface, it was an innocent enough question.

"While I keep the books, I'm by no means an expert at it." Alexander turned to bounce his gaze between his brothers, who both looked at him intently. "Stapleton Boxing Salon has been in operation for just over four months. The first two, there was much red in the ledgers, but then we'd been new at it. In the following two months, we have signed at least thirty clients, and within that number, thirty percent of them have been contracted for private lessons, which bring in more income than coming for lessons at the salon."

"Then all is well?" his mother asked with a hopeful expression.

"All is steady." Alexander took a long sip of the brandy. He winced as the liquor stung his throat. "However, during the past month following Lewis' wedding, he has been absent from the salon. Many of the men who come to the salon do so because of the chance to box or spar against him—a champion. They want to talk about our father, and Lewis is the best one with that knowledge."

"What are you trying to say, Alex?" Lewis asked with a warning growl in his voice.

Well, damn. He hadn't meant to bring this up so soon and certainly not within this company, but there was nothing for it. Turning the full force of his attention on his older brother, he sighed. "The fact of the matter is this. The moment you married, it is as if you've forgotten about everything else in your life." Briefly, he looked at Cecilia. "Not that you aren't worth his time, love, for you are, and you match him perfectly. Make him a better man."

Odd how the right woman had the power to do that.

The new countess nodded. "I take no offense, for I have said something along the same lines as you. I, too, feel he needs to divide his time between me and the salon, and since we haven't gone on a wedding trip, there is no excuse."

"Especially since this business venture is still quite new," Alexander finished with a nod. "And it was your idea to begin with as a way to fill the family coffers. The men wishing to have lessons taught by a Stapleton brother by and large want you, Lewis. Whether you like it or not, your name is well known to most people who are interested in bare-knuckle boxing; they come to be instructed by you, and when days go by without your presence in the salon, crowds flag."

"To say nothing of the fact you completely ignored Alexander at his bout last week," Duncan said into the silence that followed. "We started the salon together; we should continue in that same vein. If we all chase are own pursuits, the salon will fail."

Alexander rushed to add on another tidbit. "That isn't to say the salon should be the *only* thing of importance in any of our lives. However, since it *is* a new business, we all need to put a good bulk of our time and energy into making it a success." Pausing to sip his brandy, he then blew out a breath. "I am sacrificing my time and patience by continuing to work on the ledgers even though I'm not good at it nor do I enjoy it. You can make a sacrifice as well."

Duncan cleared his throat. "At least until such time that the salon can maintain self-sufficiency and you can begin spending more time with your lovely wife."

Good God, would they all be given dressing downs?

When he assumed his brother would bluster and yell, Lewis nodded and appeared to think over the suggestions and accusations. He nodded. "I think you are correct, Alex, and let me apologize for being absent. I shall make a point to be in the salon for at least half of each day. Would that satisfy some of your complaints?"

"For me, yes." Alexander nodded and glanced at Duncan. "What about you?"

His youngest brother shrugged. "It would be a good change."

Something deep inside prodded Alexander to speak up and advocate for himself. "At some point going forward, I would like to move away from doing the books for the salon and try my hand at managing the business, which would allow me a more hands-on approach. I could help all aspects of the salon run more efficiently if I didn't have to struggle with the ledgers and accounts. And it would allow you to move away from that and into taking over private lessons."

Silence met that statement, and as knots formed in his gut, Lewis finally nodded.

"We shall talk about that later, but you've brought up good points that will have me thinking differently on how we run the salon." He offered a tight grin. "Thank you for the insights."

He let his breath ease from his chest as relief flowed through him. "You're welcome. I think if we shift responsibilities between the three of us, everyone will have more leisure time and feel happier with the tasks we're working on."

"Impressive, brother," Duncan said with that same sentiment reflecting in his eyes. "You've changed, somehow. No longer are you a pushover, or unwilling to voice an opinion that might ruffle feathers."

"You are correct, Duncan," Lewis agreed. He then drained the brandy from his glass as he rested his gaze on Alexander. "There *is* something different about our brother." Interest lit his eyes while surprise lined their mother's face. "What have you been occupied with of late?"

Oh, dear God.

Alexander shook his head. "Nonsense. I'm the same man that I've always been."

"No, there *is* something distinctly different now." Duncan stood up from the low sofa while the ladies looked on with fascination. "I noticed it in the past two weeks. You've grown bolder as if you have found new confidence, as if you are secure in the knowledge that someone is in your corner, fighting for you, supporting you." One of his brown eyebrows cocked as he came toward Alexander. "So what is it?"

"Or rather, *who* is it?" Lewis asked as he scrambled to his feet as well.

Of course, their mother was caught up in the excitement. "Alexander? What are they hinting at?" Then she gasped. "Are the rumors circulating about the *beau monde* true? *Do* you have a woman in your life?"

Well, shit.

With four pairs of eyes on him, all full of expectation, he blew out a breath. After downing the remaining contents of his glass and suffering the burn in his throat, he rested the vessel on the fireplace mantel. "Yes."

The ladies gasped.

Lewis frowned. "Is it that same woman who came by the salon the other day? The daughter of the doctor who comes out to the boxing bouts sometimes?"

"Yes." Heat went up the back of his neck. "I met her at that bout last week, and we shared a bit of a connection." He shrugged. "She expressed an interest in sparring—while still maintaining that boxing for sport or coin is a largely nodcock idea—and as we spent time together talking, a friendship of sorts formed."

Duncan laughed and then elbowed him in the ribcage. "Of sorts. We all know what that means."

"Do shut up." Alexander ignored the continued heat on his neck. They didn't need to be privy to what kind of relationship he currently enjoyed with Lydia. "In any event, I told her that in order to continue to be in her company, we needed to keep the scandal to a minimum, and I didn't wish to sneak about merely to see her." He shrugged, for what difference did it make? "I asked if I could pay my addresses to her."

Another round of gasping issued from the ladies.

His mother put a hand to her throat. "Does this mean you have entered into a courtship with this woman? That you wish to marry her?"

"Uh, as I've told Duncan and Lewis, don't rush my fences. This is quite new and in the beginning stages. I don't wish to spook her, for Miss Tetford is not anchored to the idea of being married."

His mother frowned. "Then why are you wasting your time on her when you could pursue someone else?"

Hoping for patience, Alexander shoved the fingers of one hand through his hair. "Not that I owe any of you an explanation, Miss Tetford is fascinating as well as worthy of admiration. She's determined and brave, she has clear-cut goals, and she would like to be a physician like her father."

"That is hardly the things society values. Is Miss Tetford a woman of integrity?"

"She very much is."

The frown on his mother's face deepened. "Since Lewis was unable to land an heiress or a lady of independent means—no offense, dear," she said to Cecilia, who exchanged a speaking glance with Lewis, "there is much pressure on your shoulders to make an advantageous match. I am not certain chasing after a woman who sounds rather fast and who snubs traditional roles is the best thing for you."

Of course she would say that. Annoyance rose in a hot tide to fill Alexander's chest. How much should he tell his mother? Perhaps if she knew at least some of the story, she would be more likely to accept Lydia. "In that vein, Lydia was engaged before." His mother would find that out anyway the moment she wagged her tongue to her friends. "Apparently, the man was abusive toward her and refused to support her dreams, so her reputation is a bit dented in society's eyes, but that doesn't mean she is a bad person."

"Well, it's enough that she shares at least some affection for you," his mother said with a nod. "It will be lovely to have married, and lovelier still to have a physician in the family. I'll need to invite her father and mother to dinner."

Hell's bells. "Her mother died a few years ago."

"Oh, dear. Well, who are her people? Perhaps she has aunts and uncles."

"I'm not certain. It hasn't come up in conversation, but I do know that her mother was Scottish."

Shock lined his mother's face. "Oh, Alexander. She's of Scottish blood?"

"Yes, and she has the temper to match. It's quite refreshing to interact with a woman who doesn't play games or talk in hints." Best to be honest about everything. "Her father has been invited as a guest lecturer at Cambridge for the fall term, and she has a brother who is also a physician. From what I understand, Ian works with wounded and maimed soldiers who have returned home or are indigent." While it was a noble cause, he wasn't sure his mother would see it that way. "Frankly, I am not certain that Lydia is interested in marriage. Because of this, I promised that this courtship period could be as long or as short as she wished, and if at any time, she felt we wouldn't suit, we could terminate it with no animosity."

"What a noble thing to do, Alexander." Respect shone in Cecilia's eyes. "No doubt Miss Tetford appreciates that small consideration, for no woman should be forced into doing something she either doesn't want or isn't ready for. That bit of freedom might work to your advantage later."

"Thank you." He welcomed any support from his family, even if it was from the extended branch. "It is much like having a skittish horse become accustomed to me. I don't wish to break her spirit or crush her dreams; I just want her to trust me enough to realize I'm not like most men."

The silence following that statement was stunning, and it only stirred the insecurities still lurking in his chest.

"I admire you, brother," Duncan said as he clapped a hand on Alexander's shoulder. "You'll no doubt win her over with patience and understanding. And Mama, you'll need to square with the fact that Miss Tetford is quite forthright and stubborn. Perhaps she'll stand up to you, and that is what we've all been waiting for."

While Duncan and Lewis chuckled, Alexander focused on his mother.

"Please say that you will reserve judgment until I can determine where the relationship is headed. It is uncharted territory for me, but all I can say is that when I'm with her, she makes me want to be better, in all the ways that matter." Would that admission make him seem weak in his brothers' eyes?

His mother cleared her throat as she slowly rose to her feet. "I will have you know that I'm not the apparent ogre you boys consider me, and as a matter of fact, Cecilia has already stood up to me quite handily." She smiled at the new countess, then at Lewis, before resting her gaze back on Alexander. "I am quite glad my sons have the discernment to choose women who have backbones even if they aren't the darlings of the *ton*."

"Ah, a backhanded compliment. I didn't expect anything less

from you, Mama," he said but with enough humor in his voice to let her know he wasn't angry.

"I mean well." She nodded. "Bring Miss Tetford to the ball my friend is throwing in a few days. Lewis has been invited. He's bringing Cecilia, but I want you to come as well. I shall inform my friend you'll come with Miss Tetford."

It was his turn to frown, for this would be the first official society event he attended with Lydia for all the *ton* to see them together. "Why would you do this?" If she was expecting Lydia to fail, he would refuse outright.

"Because I want to see you happy, Alexander. As much as I would like for my boys to have financial stability, your father didn't leave us well off, but there are more important things than how much coin a person has to their name." She laid a hand on his arm. "Also, you can find out much about a person while on a dance floor. Come to the ball. If she can't deport herself correctly or the two of you don't flow together while waltzing, you'll have your answer." Then she laid a palm against his cheek. "I'll have a quick conversation with her as well, but don't worry, I just want to make certain she is good enough for you." She bussed his cheek. "Besides, all of my sons clean up well and make lovely impressions when dressed for a ball. If she doesn't fall for you then, she is obviously not the one."

Oddly, it made sense. He nodded just as the butler entered the room and rang a hand bell announcing that dinner was ready. "Thank you. I shall invite her tomorrow and will hope for the best."

Chapter Thirteen

August 16, 1817
No. 16
Grosvenor Square, Mayfair
London, England

"PAPA, WE NEED to talk."

Lydia came into her father's study as the longcase clock on the floor above chimed the midday hour. All through breakfast, she'd worried and wondered as her mind spun with confliction and confusion.

"Poppet, is all well?" Immediately, he rose from to his feet and came around his desk of cherrywood, because of course being a physician, he would draw the worst conclusions. "Has something happened?"

"No. Everything is well; I am fine." The poor, dear man. She waved him back into his chair as she settled into one of the comfortable leather ones in front of his desk. They had been in each study of every home they'd lived in since her father had become a doctor. "I haven't spent much time with you over the past couple of weeks."

"My schedule has been uncommonly busy, but I appreciate your assistance with my patients. And I can't help that my social calendar is also full." He frowned as he rested his gaze on her. "There is something else, though, isn't there? It has nothing to do with patients or the practice."

"Well, it does in a roundabout way, I suppose." And perhaps it was a good way to ease into the conversation. "I know you have been wanting to expand your patient base into a space that is larger than the office you have now, so I've been looking around. There is a spot for let in a building on Brook Street, near the Stapleton Boxing Salon that I think you should inquire about. It would allow for a more efficient practice, and I could take the lead when you are out at Cambridge for your lectures."

"I appreciate the insight. Perhaps tomorrow you and I can convince the owner to give us a tour." He steepled his fingers, then rested his hands on the papers spread over his desktop. "However, I'll wager that is not what's truly on your mind or why you sought me out."

Mild heat filled her cheeks. "It is not."

Her father nodded. "What did you wish to talk about then?"

Did she even know herself? "I fear it's quite complicated."

"The most important things in our life usually are, or that is what our minds tell us, when in reality, we only think that." He grinned, and his eyes were kind. "We tell ourselves those important notions are complicated as a way to talk ourselves out of pursuing them, for we assume that they will cause too much work or too much heartbreak."

"What if the worry is caused by neither of those options?"

"Then I'll encourage you to continue thinking about it and go deeper, for it will always be one of those things." Once more, he stood up and came around the desk, but this time he settled into the leather chair that matched hers. "It's not often you come to me for advice. Even from a young age, you knew exactly what you wanted from life and how to go about chasing it."

She allowed herself a small smile. "This is true."

"And not even once did you allow your mother's suggestions on learning the skills a society lady should know distract you." When she didn't answer, her father sighed. "So why do I have a feeling you have something—or someone—that you now consider a threat to the trajectory of your life *in* that life? And you don't know what to do about it?"

"How do you know me so well?"

He shrugged. "I've known you all your life, and have been with you every step of the way." Compassion shadowed his eyes. "Can I assume that you are worried over a certain boxer you met at that bout two weeks ago? The same man that keeps a blush in your cheeks and a sparkle in your eyes each time you come home?"

Oh, dear.

She blew out a breath. "How much do you know or perhaps suspect?"

"Very little, so it would help if you started at the beginning." When he reached out and took one of her hands in his, tears sprang into her eyes, for it reminded her of when she was a little girl and would come to him for advice. "And remember, there is no shame in changing your mind on certain things, if that is what's happening."

"I don't know, and that's why all of this is so confusing!" Spending a few seconds trying to order her emotions, Lydia finally sighed. "I met Viscount Wexley at that bout you and I attended."

"Yes, I know, and I also saw you initiate a kiss at that time as well."

The heat in her cheeks intensified. "What can I say? He is quite attractive, and I wanted to know what it would feel like."

"You were always quite progressive in your thinking and actions, much to your mother's embarrassment, but only when she wanted you to be a society lady." He winked. "All the other times, she was inordinately proud of you for standing up for what you believed."

"I miss her so much," Lydia whispered as she clung to her father's hand. "Talking to her would have been such a comfort right now." She pressed her lips together as she thought about her next words. "Suffice it to say, I have been going by Stapleton's

Boxing Salon regularly to see Lord Wexley, or rather Alexander. He has been giving me boxing lessons, which is a good thing since Colin has now come to London and has taken to following me about and trying to physically encourage me to give him another chance."

"In other words, he's attacked you." Her father's expression turned to a thundercloud.

"Yes." She nodded. "The first time, you were at a society function, and I couldn't locate Ian, so I sent a missive to Alexander and asked that he come to call because I didn't wish to be alone." And the aftermath of that visit was still so lovely and fresh in her mind that tingles of renewed need fell down her spine. With a little shiver, she continued. "In any event, he has indicated an interest in paying his addresses to me."

"Oh?" His eyebrows rose with surprise. "And you are allowing that?"

"I am, only in as far as to discover if we would even suit."

"Does he realize you aren't the world's greatest supporter of marriage?"

"He does… and he keeps coming 'round anyway."

"How interesting." Her father squeezed her fingers. "I'm impressed with his determination even if it means he'll be ultimately disappointed once matters between you grow intense."

"Ah, Papa." Lydia shook her head as emotions rose into her throat. "It already has, and this relationship is so confusing, because he is not behaving as I would expect a man to, as I have already seen men act." She raised his hand and pressed his palm to her cheek. "But Alexander is nothing like those men, and what is more, he shows it time and time again. He is always there, telling me I'm not alone, reassuring me that he will support me in whatever decisions I wish to make should the two of us continue the courtship."

"I'm afraid I don't understand where the complication comes in," her father said with a grin that indicated he did, indeed, know, but just wanted her to say it aloud.

She huffed, and ruffled a few curls on her forehead. "As much as I've spoken out against the ills that come along with marriage and the very real threat of losing my freedom if I fall victim to that state, I... Well, I fear I'm starting to fall for the viscount. Soon, it won't be long until I lose my heart to him, and that terrifies me."

"Why? From everything you've said, he sounds like the perfect match for you. Not overbearing or brash but not a pushover who won't let you walk all over him."

"Because it might mean that I was wrong. About marriage, and about everything else in my life, so what if I was wrong about wishing to be a doctor?" She pulled away, but he stilled her by taking her hand in his again. "I have never known that I wanted to do anything else in my life other than healing people who are hurting."

"But what about healing yourself, poppet? Your heart needs attention the same as anyone else." For long moments, they were silent before he spoke again. "Does he make you happy?"

"I'm beginning to suspect that he does. He is funny and charming, has a head for business, and if he will learn how to stand up for himself against his family, I think he could really make a difference at the boxing salon." She shook her head. "As much as I adore appreciating his form—"

Her father held up a hand, palm outward. "I don't wish to hear about that," he interrupted with a cheeky grin.

Heat sank into her cheeks once more. "He is a passable boxer, and he persists in having the dream that he'll continue to enter bouts for the purpose of winning a prize purse, but I fear he will be hurt beyond my skill in fixing him one of these days." Knots of worry pulled in her belly. "I understand that he wishes to sort his future in the event he does want marriage, yet why can't he understand that I don't need anything fancy or luxurious, and instead, I only need..."

"...him," her father said in a soft voice with a nod of encouragement. "You only need him. And that no doubt frightens you too, because up until now, you have been quite self-sufficient in your life. You've done everything yourself, relied on yourself. Now you must consider his feelings and his dreams, figure out how they might fit in with yours, and you wonder if you'll suddenly be subsumed within that."

"Yes, there is that, of course, but what if I truly do want marriage with him when all is said and done?"

"That isn't a crime, poppet, especially if you love him."

"And I'm terrified of what might happen should I fall pregnant."

Her father nodded. "I suppose being trained as a physician doesn't help with that, but even with the knowledge of everything that can go wrong, there is more than enough hope that things will go right." Again, he took her hand. "Don't let fretting about what might happen in the future take away from the happiness or joy there is to be found in life now."

"That is good advice, but what if I end up falling in love with him?"

"Aw, poppet, I would be pleased, for that would mean you wouldn't be alone."

"No." She shook her head. How to explain? "I mean, to his own admission, Alexander has said he doesn't have much coin to set up housekeeping, and—"

"Then you can enjoy a long engagement. If he is as strong and dedicated as you say, I'll wager he'll be quick in figuring things out, especially if he knows a life with you is in the offing." When she didn't say anything but stared at him, her father sighed. "We can't always be guaranteed of anything, but that doesn't mean we should shy away from the things that make life worth living merely because we don't know how any of it will be accomplished."

"Is that what you felt with Mama?"

"Good heavens, yes. An English man from a good family falling in love with a Scottish healer whose parents were laborers? Yes, there were always doubts, but in the end, love won. Love always wins over every doubt, every fear, every rift or excuse our minds can find to keep it from that." He patted her hand. "When you don't know which way to go, always follow love. It will never steer you wrong."

"But I—"

"Here is the truth. If thinking about this man has you all tied up in knots and your mind in a quagmire of opposing thoughts, there is a good chance he just might be the man you've waited for all this time."

"Well, he did defend me against Colin the other day when the oaf followed us into Hyde Park." A tremulous smile curved her lips. "And he really is a darling when he does anything…" As she met her father's eyes, an unexpected giggle escaped her throat. "So then, you believe I'm in a spot of bother too?"

"Just slightly. If he's willing to let you have *cart blanche* in in a possible blended future, you need to latch onto him and not let him go." He laughed, and when he stood, he brought her up with him. "I would like to meet your young man, so invite him to dinner one of the nights I'll be home. That way, I can ask him a few questions and see for myself how the two of you interact with each other."

"But Papa I—"

"No excuses, poppet. If Lord Wexley is as lovely as you seem to think—when you're not trying to talk yourself out of liking him—then there is no reason to fear the two of us meeting." He winked.

"Oh, it's all so very frightening. Perhaps I should just call everything off before it goes any deeper." And it would save her from being disappointed. "I am only six and twenty. There is no need to pursue marriage at this time."

"Hush, poppet. There is every reason, especially if love is involved. Don't cheat yourself from one of the best things in life due to fear, for there will always be that before every change in life."

Drat, but that made sense.

"Besides, he and I will need to build some sort of friendship, especially since I'll be expecting him to call and ask me for your hand more sooner than later. Even if you do have the tendency to be a managing baggage. Does he know that about you?"

"Do stop, Papa." She couldn't help but laugh. "I suppose I am a *tad* forthright when we are together."

"Now *that* I can believe."

"That is only because I can see so much potential in him." She snorted. "He doesn't seem to mind."

"The good ones don't. In fact, we'll encourage it."

"Is that what happened with you and Mama?"

"Oh, yes, and we rubbed along just fine. Mutual support is a wonderful thing, and quite a vital component to a successful union." He grinned. "With her, I felt as if I could do or be anything, and was rather reckless each time she smiled."

Even more did Lydia miss her mother. "But we are nowhere near *that* point yet." Except heat fired in her cheeks, and the thought of being wed to Alexander had butterflies dancing through her insides.

What has happened to me?

"Well, poppet, I suppose we definitely need to go look at the space to let near that boxing salon, hmm? And it would make sense to be located closely to such an establishment in the event some of those practice bouts grow out of hand." He winked, then bundled her into a hug that once more had her remembering how safe he'd made her feel when she was a girl. "Speaking of boxing, I've been engaged to be the consulting physician for an illegal bout in a few days. Would you have any interest in accompanying me?"

"That depends. Are any of the Stapleton brothers on the schedule?" As far as she knew, Alexander wasn't booked to fight in a bout.

"Not that I'm aware of, but fighters change on the schedule all the time for many reasons." He pulled back with a laugh. "You might find a man you fancy more than the handsome viscount."

"Papa, stop!" With a chuckle of her own, Lydia shook her head. "One man in my life is quite enough, thank you." She then glanced at the clock on his desk. "Goodness, but I'm going to be late. I'm due at the salon soon. Both the earl and the younger Stapleton are due out this afternoon, and Alexander has promised that we'd have the salon all to ourselves." Another round of heat went into her cheeks as one of her father's eyebrows rose in question. "Not for that sort of activity, but for a boxing lesson that includes sparring. However, I plan to teach him a few moves in jujitsu, and I can't wait to see his surprise when I knock him onto his back."

Additionally, it would set his mind at ease that she could defend herself against another attack from Colin should one arise. And if he were already lying on a tick mattress, it would be all the easier to convince him to indulge in other… activities.

"Please promise you will be careful. Society's gossips are vicious. If they get wind of you stepping foot into a boxing salon, Alexander's fighting in a bout again will be the least of your worries." He blew out a breath. "Obviously, I'm not happy you're going there, but I also know I can't stop you."

"I'll be mindful." She put a palm to his cheek then bussed his other one. "Will I see you and Ian for dinner?"

"Actually, yes. It's a rare evening when we will all be home."

"Good." She grinned. "Perhaps I can convince Lord Wexley to join us." Then, with a wave, she left his study. Good heavens, was she truly ready to introduce Alexander to her family? Only time would tell, but it was the next logical step. If her father and brother didn't get along with him, then she would know he wasn't the one for her.

Wouldn't she?

Chapter Fourteen

August 17, 1817
Stapleton Boxing Salon
Mayfair, London

S INCE IT WAS a Sunday, the boxing salon was closed today, and that gave Alexander both relief and a bit of sadness, for usually having clients on the floor gave him renewed energy. However, he came into the salon regardless, because he had ledgers to balance and a few vendor invoices to pay.

He hadn't seen Lydia for a couple of days, and if he were honest with himself, he missed her presence in his life. After he'd talked with his family regarding her, his outlook for the future had been infused with even more confidence, regardless that the doctor's daughter wasn't exactly marriage-minded. Could he convince her to take a chance, that all would be well, when he didn't even know that? Only time would tell.

An hour after he settled into his accounting duties, rain drummed against the windows, and it provided a pleasant background to his work. As the candle flame danced, shadows moved over his ledger pages, but it was oddly soothing while he concentrated on the numbers.

No sooner had he finished one task than a bold knock on the office door interrupted him.

"What the devil?" He stood. When he opened the door and

spied Lydia on the narrow landing, he frowned, for she wore an expression of concern that wrinkled her forehead. "Is everything well?"

"I'm not certain. Might I come in?"

He stood back from the door. "Do you want another boxing lesson?"

"No." She shook her head. "I wanted to talk with you, and since I obviously couldn't go to your rooms at The Albany, I took a chance that you might be here… without your brothers." As she proceeded into the room, she untied the satin ribbons of her bonnet from beneath her chin and then removed the headgear as Alexander closed the door. "It started to rain, and since it is rather bothersome being wet—again—I came here directly."

"Well, as you said not long ago, being wet isn't a bad thing," he told her with a wink. "I'm afraid I don't have tea to offer you, but I can call for my brother's closed carriage and perhaps go to a tearoom."

"I don't require tea. At least not right at this moment." Once she'd removed her ivory spencer, she draped it over the end of a leather sofa. "Since when has there been a sofa in this office?"

"Oh." Alexander glanced at the piece of furniture nestled beneath the windows, across the room from the tick mattresses. "Lewis took his wife's advice. She wanted somewhere to sit when she visited him, somewhere she could read while he worked, or do whatever it is that women do when waiting on a man."

God, I sound like an utter nodcock.

At least it prompted a faint smile on her part, and his gaze dropped briefly to her mouth. "It is actually a good idea." So saying, Lydia took a seat on the middle of the three cushions. Once she removed her gloves, she laid them on the cushion beside her. "I came because we *do* need to talk."

"I agree."

"You do?" Surprise clouded her eyes.

"Yes." He nodded. "Further, I believe it's long overdue." Could he find his courage and tell her what he was beginning to feel? Would it make a difference?

"Perhaps it is." After taking the reticule from her wrist, she tossed it to a corner of the sofa. "The night you came to dinner at my house—"

"Two nights ago, at your father's behest?" That had been an interesting evening wherein the good doctor had asked him a few pointed questions, but overall, it had been lovely to meet Lydia's family.

"Yes." It was her turn to nod. "Well, before dinner, I had a long chat with him regarding you." Instead of meeting his gaze, she kept her attention focused on her hands in her lap. "I needed his counsel about certain… things."

He frowned. "Why?"

"Since meeting you, my mind has been besieged with confusion, and I've found myself second-guessing my decisions. Decisions, I might add, that I have never before wavered upon since making them. All because of you." Finally, she raised her gaze, and the emotions she spoke of were reflected in her eyes.

"What?" Caught once more by shock, Alexander sat—or rather collapsed—on the cushion beside her. "I have never once asked that you change anything about yourself on my behalf." Is that what she'd told her father? Is that why the man was so interested in questioning him at dinner the other night?

"I know you haven't, and quite frankly, you've been everything lovely and strong and you've appealed to my wild, baser instincts, which is quite a distraction."

"Then why do you seem so devastated by that?"

"Because it is something that needs to be done… I think." Her eyes looked stricken, as if she'd come to a particularly horrible decision. "I have come here to tell you that entering into a courtship with you was a mistake, and that we are not a good match for each other." Tears echoed in her voice. "So while I have had a lovely time with you, I believe we are better as acquaintances."

"I beg your pardon, but what the hell, Lydia?" Hurt and betrayal slammed into his chest, but overall, he was shocked and a bit panicked. "From my perspective, things were progressing quite well between us, so where is this sudden digging in of your heels coming from?" In fact, his chest tightened to the point that he had trouble breathing. When she didn't answer—or wouldn't—he shook his head as the truth dawned. "You are afraid because you fancy me just enough that you have been thinking about a future with me."

"No, that's not it. I…"

The fact she couldn't finish the sentence gave credence to his guess. His suddenly flagging spirits took flight. "You, my dear, are a terrible liar. Your having feelings for me terrifies you, so you've decided to push me away, to put distance between us that will keep you from being hurt, for you have managed to convince yourself that I won't let you be who you are even though I've promised you that many times."

Now that he'd identified the problem, he could talk her through it. All wasn't as lost as he'd feared.

The delicate tendons in her throat worked with a hard swallow. "It isn't just me who I'm trying not to hurt; it's you as well." She shook her head while tears welled in her eyes. "You are a good man, Alexander, and you don't deserve to have a woman at your side who isn't society's definition of a good match."

"Such gammon. I also never said I wanted the perfect or ideal wife." He held her gaze. Never had he been so close to having everything he'd had no idea he wanted. "Talk to me, Lydia. Tell me what you're thinking instead of shutting me out."

"No." When she would have stood up from the sofa, he grabbed her hand and kept her in place. "You'll simply ply me with charm and then I'll change my mind."

"As well you should, because this is a stupid plan." Thinking that she needed extra encouragement, Alexander tugged her into his arms, holding her tight against his chest. "You attracted me from the start with your forthright attitude and your unorthodox views. I *stayed* interested with your plain speaking and your unwavering desire to follow your dreams, no matter that everything about that goes against everything society wants from a woman."

"I can no more give up being a physician any more than you can give up being a boxer." Her words were slightly muffled by his cravat.

"There is no reason that you should. I am not that sort of man, and I'd hoped I'd given you ample reasons to see that."

For long moments, she remained quiet before nodding. "But if we continue in this vein and follow the courtship to its inevitable conclusion, this will mean your name will constantly be in the gossip mill due to my penchant for thumbing my nose at society. You might be shunned or cut out of receiving invitations or perhaps will lose clients."

"Ha." He pulled back slightly in order to peer into her face. The shining hope there knocked him for a loop. "For too long you've pushed people away before they could either disappoint you or demand that you give up your notions of living life on your own terms. Is this correct?"

She sighed. "How can you possibly know that?" A hint of annoyance threaded through her voice.

"I have spent enough time with you to know what sort of woman you are, what kind of woman you will always be, and it humbles the hell out of me at times."

"Humbles you?"

He nodded. "Pushes me to be better in every aspect of my life. Is that easier to swallow?

"And that doesn't bother you?"

"God, no. In fact, it *thrills* me. Do you truly believe I value any of those things you mentioned over sharing a potential future with you?" One of his eyebrows arched. "I do not. And the invitations you think will stop?" He snorted with derision. "My brother is the Earl of Lethbridge. I am the Viscount of Wexley. My father was a lauded prize fighter. Those connections will *always* be there, and I'll move through society as much as I ever have… or haven't, depending on my mood. Besides, I shall have you, and that is what I have wanted above all else."

Her eyes rounded. The same longing, the same *yearning* circling through his chest reflected in those green depths. "Truly?"

"Absolutely. More than anything I want you in my life, Lydia."

"You barely know me."

"Whose fault is that, Miss Busy Physician?"

A blush stained her cheeks. "Yesterday, my father and I toured the space in the building next door to this one to see if it would suit for expanding his practice."

"Will it?"

"I believe so. Then there will only be an alleyway separating you and me on a regular basis."

And the temptation would accelerate. "If you think that will keep me from you, then you aren't the intelligent doctor I know you to be." He tucked an escaped lock of hair behind her ear. "Doctor's daughter, damned stubborn Scottish healer, managing baggage, unorthodox young woman, all those things are merely labels that allow you to hide, so you won't be hurt when people call you such. But I see deeper, and I know that when your heart is engaged, you will be all those things and more, just as fate has always planned for you when it set out this path for you, and I'll be standing at the side, waiting for you to finally acknowledge me, waiting for you to open your eyes and see me for the man that I am. I'm by no means perfect, but I'm trying my best."

If that didn't win her back after this temporary loss of faith or confidence, then nothing would.

"Oh, Alexander, you are perfect to me—*for* me!" Lydia shifted positions and threw herself into his arms with enough force that he toppled backward with her resting haphazardly over his chest and his head went onto the bolstered end of the sofa. "I am rubbish with navigating through life when emotions are involved."

He couldn't help but chuckle. "That, my dear, is a rather large understatement. I am struggling with the same."

"It makes me glad to know I'm not alone." Her purr of laughter went straight to his member, and damn if that organ didn't harden to painful awareness. "We're all broken and jagged, I think, trying to make sense of life and find lasting connections therein. But when we find somewhere that we are accepted and understood? When we find someone who feels like home? There is nothing to describe that."

"That sums it all up quite nicely." Home. She felt like home to him. Alexander ran his hands up and down her arms as she levered into a sitting position straddling his waist. "Now, do you need more convincing that this courtship is still the best thing for both of us?"

"Possibly. You know how stubborn I am, and not easily impressed." When she grinned and the gesture crinkled the delicate skin at the corners of her eyes, he lost another piece of his heart to her.

"That's all the encouragement I need to show you that I am, indeed, the man for you, and if I'm not, there is no doubt that you'll tell me how I can improve." He slipped a hand to her nape, tugged her down, and then kissed her with enthusiasm as if he hadn't seen her for years instead of a mere two days. Those soft petal lips welcomed him home without condition or exception.

It was one of the best things about falling in love, or so he assumed, since he'd never truly been in such a state before.

Minutes later, she broke the embrace to smile at him. The bodice of her dress gaped, for he'd undone the laces at the back and the sleeves had slipped down her arms. The fabric clung to her breasts with barely a breath, and damn if that wasn't the most erotic thing he'd ever seen. "Does that mean we shall continue with the courtship?"

"Yes, but I still have those fears."

"We both do, but those feelings are merely gatekeepers. They are there to help you make certain the thing you want on the other side of them is exactly what is written on your heart."

"What a lovely way of explaining it. Thank you, and… I think it might be."

Though he wished to shout his potential happiness from the rooftop, that would mean tearing himself away from the wonders of this woman's arms, and quite honestly, he'd rather worship her body than go out into the rain.

"I try. God how I try."

"You do, and there is a certain elegance to that." Lydia's eyes darkened with the same desire that currently lit tiny fires in his blood. "What did you have in mind, then, for this afternoon, Wexley?" One of her finely feathered red eyebrows arched in invitation or challenge, he couldn't decide, but knowing her, it was a challenge.

Was there any wonder he was coming to adore her? "Perhaps it's better I show you. Words you might not believe since any man can utter them, but actions will stay with you longer."

"Such a quick study." She lowered her head to his. "That is *quite* an attractive quality." Then she kissed him.

And his world fell apart.

Their tongues met and tangled in a mating dance as old as time. In short order, he stripped to his breeches and lawn shirt. Her dress joined the growing pile of discarded clothing, as did her stays and petticoat. Fingers and hands were seemingly everywhere; caresses encouraged moans and questing fingertips over sensitive skin were met with gasps and sighs. It took little time to remove his shirt and her chemise, and once she was gloriously naked, Alexander laid her on the sofa and came over her.

"Perhaps bringing in a sofa was a good idea after all," he whispered against her soft skin.

"Agreed." And she drew her fingers along his chest, leaving maddening sensations behind.

Giddy awareness assailed him as he kissed a path down her body, being sure to tease and torment her nipples as he went. Her back arched; she furrowed her fingers into his hair while he continued his quest to lick and nibble every inch of her. When he pressed his lips to her mons, she splayed her thighs, wriggled her hips in invitation, and Alexander didn't need another clue.

How damned fortunate am I when I'm with her?

He devoured her, showed her with his tongue and fingers how he would claim her in mere moments. Whimpering cries of need left her throat and still he explored. Soon enough he encouraged her swollen nubbin out of hiding. There was a certain satisfaction in knowing he would have many times in the future to perfect how to work her body in ways that would bring maximum pleasure. Through suction and friction, he brought her to the edge of bliss again and again. By the time she came undone from his ministrations, he was hard to the point of discomfort, needed to join with her else he'd embarrass himself.

On the brand-new sofa, and he'd never hear the end of it from Lewis.

While Lydia was lost to the throes of her release, he left the sofa long enough to remove his breeches. By the time her breathing had returned to normal, and a red flush swept over her upper chest, he'd again covered her body with his and claimed her lips.

But she apparently wasn't in the mood to be courted. She looped her arms about his shoulders, and as she pulled him closer, she wrapped her legs around his, holding him in the cradle of her hips. "I need you, Alexander." The whisper was fraught with desire and a touch desperate.

"You have me, for as long as you want." Would that translate to marriage if he might ask soon? Only the gods knew, but he remained hopeful. He kissed her again because he could, and feathered his fingers into her hair to gently hold her head in his palm, keeping her steady. With his other hand, he guided his shaft, teasing her flesh with his tip before thrusting, taking her, claiming her, spearing into her, and he didn't stop until he'd buried himself stones deep. Sensations raced along every nerve ending; a rush of tingling awareness went over him.

"Damn, but this moment is one of my favorite things."

Lydia moaned with delight. "You are… Well, there is no one like you." She squirmed beneath him, taking him ever deeper. As she tightened her inner muscles, squeezing his length, she lightly bit his earlobe. "For the love of all that's holy, please continue. I have thought of nothing except coupling with you since the last time."

"In this, you and I are of one accord."

Then, he moved slowly in and out of her passage for the sheer pleasure of feeling that glide. As if they'd known each other for a lifetime, they settled upon a rhythm that was much like dancing. Alexander gripped her hips, canting them at an angle he preferred and one that would give her the most pleasure. She threw her head back, and with each new thrust, sounds of encouragement left her throat.

"This is… You are…" She gasped. "I'm afraid we won't know how to act when we have the opportunity to do this in a bed."

"Perhaps we are enough different that we don't need to follow the rules even in this," he whispered back, for he couldn't distract himself from his task.

This coupling was more than a quick joining that had no purpose other than to culminate in physical pleasure. No, now he made love to her, the woman he hoped to win at the end of this courtship, the woman he would gladly pledge his life to, the woman he feared he was coming to love in such a short period of time.

Then the pace of his thrusts changed as frantic need tingled through his stones and shaft. Deeper still he plunged. Faster he worked his hips. Harder he stroked in an effort to send her flying while denying himself the same satisfaction, if only for a moment. Lydia strained beneath him, her back arching, the perfect globes of her breasts bouncing, her skin flushing with arousal. As he switched his angle of penetration and the root of his shaft rubbed against her swollen nubbin, the first frantic cry broke the silence.

With gasps and words of approval, she fell into bliss so completely the contractions of her channel yanked him into a release immediately. White light rushed up to meet him, and for a few seconds he existed in a void where there was nothing except the rapid tattoo of his pulse and the labored sound of his breathing, while the warmth of her exhalations skated across his cheek.

As he murmured words that had no meaning or even structure, Alexander collapsed on top of her, and she wrapped her arms around him. He kissed the side of her neck, her cheeks that were salty from tears, her closed eyelids, and finally her sweat-damp forehead. With her, he would always have a supporter in his corner, and damn if he didn't feel as if he were going down swinging in the ring.

Only this time, it was for love, and that was worth fighting for.

"Thank you," he whispered against her lips.

She uttered a tiny snort. "For what?"

Let me count the ways. He brushed his lips against hers while holding her gaze. "For believing in me, seeing that I can be someone other than a Stapleton brother."

"Well, you are that, and forever will be. There is nothing wrong in living to honor your father's legacy, but there is something to be said for wanting to discover who you are beyond the boxing world."

"Yes, of course." He rolled onto his side and took her with him. "Did your father agree to let the space next door?"

"He did, but since he will be at Cambridge during the week until the Michaelmas term, we have decided not to do anything until then." She nuzzled the crook of his neck, and his shaft tightened all over again. "By then, perhaps I will have a more definitive direction for my future, and if the space isn't available, there will be others."

"In the event you wondered, I will be there for whatever you decide."

"I am beginning to realize that. You have no idea how much that means to me."

And you have no idea what you *are beginning to mean to* me.

Why did men fear falling for a woman? Why had he, when it made him feel stronger than he'd ever had before? Hell, if he went into the ring tomorrow, he had every confidence he would win the bout. "My mother wishes for me to attend a ball thrown by one of her friends in two days. I know it's short notice, but would you come with me?" How much did he want to dance with her, show her off to society as his?

Her eyes rounded. "Are you certain?"

"Yes." As he slipped a hand over her hip, he grinned. "Do you have a ballgown?"

"Of course. I'm not quite a country bumpkin. Papa allows me to have three news ones done up a year. I promise I'll behave myself with a winsome air and modest deportment," she said with a wicked twinkle in her eye.

"Don't you dare. I want the *ton* to see why I have been distracted beyond all reason by a doctor's daughter with Scottish roots." Damn, he was proud of her. "And perhaps you can meet my mother." That would be an interesting situation. Good thing there would be brandy at hand.

Lydia sighed. "Why am I so weak-willed when it comes to you?"

"Well, I *am* addicting and charming, so there's that."

"Do hush, Wexley. No one likes a braggart." But she smiled, then slipped a hand to his nape and pulled him close for a kiss.

Life was damned near perfect.

Chapter Fifteen

August 19, 1817
No. 16
Grosvenor Square, Mayfair
London, England

L YDIA ONLY ATE random bites of her breakfast that morning. Mostly, she pushed the food about her plate, moving forkfuls of fluffy, golden, scrambled eggs from one side to the other or cutting the hamsteak into tiny, little squares.

Tonight, she would accompany Alexander to a ball hosted by one of his mother's friends. And that was why she was beset by a bad case of the nerves. Not for going out into society. She did that numerous times during the regular Season. A summer event wouldn't be any different, though there might not be as many notables in attendance since they were still enjoying leisure time at their country estates.

No, the nerves were exclusively for doing all of that at Alexander's side. Not that there was anything wrong with attending a ball. Over the past week or so, she had consented to let him court her, and they'd done a few things together where the gossips had apparently seen them. It was just that going to a ball was akin to making a direct statement.

Did she want that? She snorted as she ferried a bite of eggs to the other side of her plate. So it would seem, especially after that last coupling with the viscount. There had been emotion shared between them, as if pieces of their souls had mingled to resettle in a combined entity, as odd as it sounded. That afternoon they'd bonded, and deep down inside she knew they were irrevocably bound together, come what may.

She'd never felt that way when she'd been engaged to Colin, and while that was wildly telling, it also brought with it more second guessing as well as fear.

What if she was only deluding herself because she was trying to chase something she thought she *should* have?

"Everything will come out well in the end, you know," her father said as he came into the morning room and immediately went to the sideboard for a cup of the fragrant coffee that had been brewed.

"In reference to what?" She let her fork fall onto her plate with a clatter.

"Don't play coy, my girl. I mean Lord Wexley. That's who you're mooning about, isn't it? And that is why you suddenly have no appetite?"

Heat blazed in her cheeks. It would seem she'd become *that* sort of woman. The kind who let a man possess all the spaces of her mind when she should be thinking about things that would benefit humanity instead. "Yes, it's him I'm thinking about."

"Oh? Has something monumental occurred in your rather unorthodox relationship?" As he spoke, he came toward the round table and took a seat beside her while a footman brought over a plate with all her father's breakfast favorites upon it.

"I don't know how monumental it is." With a sigh, she pushed away her plate. There was no use pretending that she was hungry. "Two days ago, I went to the salon with the intention of breaking our courtship."

"Why?" He frowned. "Do you suddenly not suit?"

"No." With the shake of her head, she uttered another sigh. "I allowed myself to let my fears and thoughts consume me, and I panicked." When she met her father's gaze, his understanding smile disarmed her. "But Wexley sucked me back in. He used logic on me, explained to me that hiding behind my fears helped me to push people and things away so I wouldn't have a chance to be hurt or disappointed."

"He's not wrong, and it sounds as if he has good sense, as well as the wont to look after you."

"But why, though?"

"Oh, poppet." A laugh escaped him. "It means he's tip over tail for you, and if he has enough wherewithal to make you change your mind about giving up on a courtship before it's truly gotten started, there is every possibility you'll be wed to him before the year is out."

When a wave of familiar panic would have rushed through her chest, it unexpectedly died before it could take hold. In its place came a warm, gentle feeling of calm, because she knew with Alexander, everything would truly turn out right as rain if she would let it. "It's all so confusing."

"That is generally what love is, my girl. Confusing, messy, it will make you run the gambit of emotions, put you through the proverbial wringer, and then make you fly."

Love. Is that where she was headed, then? Of course it was. There was no use in denying it. "I've committed to going to a ball with him tonight."

"Wonderful!" He patted her hand. "That is a lovely first step, my girl."

"What if—"

"None of that, now. You will be amazing and look beautiful. Everyone you meet will think you lovely and a good match for Lord Wexley."

"Will you come with me?"

"I wish I could, but I have a commitment elsewhere tonight. Er, really not tonight, per say, but rather in the gloaming before dawn."

"Are you meeting clandestinely with a woman, then?" He truly did need to marry again, for he was one of those men who was happiest with a woman in his life.

"Of course not." He chuckled, then tucked into his breakfast. "Perhaps once I see you settled and married. As a matter of course, I'll be the attending physician for a bare-knuckle boxing match in the morning."

"Ah." Since Alexander hadn't mentioned anything about that to her, she assumed he wouldn't be one of the fighters, and that set her mind at ease. "Well, I hope you have fun. I would rather not see another of those bouts if I can at all help it."

His expression was difficult to read, but he wouldn't immediately meet her gaze. "If you continue on with Lord Wexley, I'll wager he'll not let go of his ties to the boxing world."

"And neither should he. That is part of who he is, but he can be so much more." She blew out a breath. "I just hope he'll do fewer of those bouts."

Her father cleared his throat. "I'm sure he can hold his own, poppet. Have some faith in your man."

"I do, of course, I just worry." Thank goodness Alexander would be with her tonight.

Willingham House
Hanover Square
Mayfair, London

AFTER CLEARING THE reception line and meeting the Marquess and Marchioness of Quince, Alexander had encouraged her to go ahead into the ballroom of the large townhouse and that he would catch her up in a few moments, for he wished to speak with his brother as well as an acquaintance or two.

"You don't wish to introduce me to them?"

"Absolutely I do, and that will occur a bit later in the evening, I promise." Then, with a wink, he'd loped away and soon disappeared into the crowded corridor.

Not wishing to socialize, Lydia stood at one of the walls while taking a few deep breaths to calm her nerves. There had been no time to compliment Alexander on his attire in the carriage, for when he'd called at her home to escort her to the ball, he'd come in an open carriage that also conveyed the Earl and Countess of Lethbridge. At least she would know another couple at the event, and she was seated on the bench next to the countess, so there had been no opportunity to speak candidly with Alexander or even try to steal a kiss.

As the first country reel got underway, she smoothed her gloved hands down the front of her gown. Made of watered green taffeta, golden sequins lined the lower hem, the short, puffed sleeves as well as the low bodice; she liked it for its glittering properties and how cooling the fabric was against her legs. The hue set off her red hair to its best advantage, and gave her pale skin a bit of color and life.

Yet Alexander hadn't said one word about her toilette to-night. Perhaps like her, he hadn't had the time or opportunity.

After what seemed like an eternity and in the middle of the second dance of the evening, the viscount finally came back to her location.

"I apologize for being away. There was something I needed to talk to Lewis and Duncan about that couldn't wait." Then he raked his gaze slowly up and down her person, and she swore she felt that as if he'd caressed her. "You put me in mind of a forest fairy or even an elf who has materialized in this ballroom exclusively for my pleasure."

Heat jumped into her cheeks from his praise. "Thank you. My maid spent a copious amount of time on my toilette. She insisted that my hair be set in an elaborate style." As she spoke, Lydia touched her tresses that had been dressed in curls and braids with gold ribbons woven through before the heavy mass had been secured with pins.

"Well, her pains were rewarded, for you are every inch a princess and easily one of the most beautiful women here tonight."

"Do stop, Wexley. That is excessive, even for you." Yet her insides threatened to turn to mush from his charm, even though she knew after studying medicine that it simply wasn't possible. "And someone could overhear."

"What if they do?" He waggled his eyebrows and dared to come closer to her a few steps. Citrus wafted to her nose from his shaving soap or cologne. "Then the gossip about us being in a romantic relationship will gain wings and sweep faster through the gathered crowd."

"Oh." Her traitorous heart fluttered. Romance and flirting were too distracting, wasn't it, or should she, for once, let herself enjoy the fall? "*Does* everyone need to know?" Yet after what they'd shared in the office of the boxing salon the other day, she had more or less committed to him, had even encouraged him to continue with his courtship, and gone so far as to tell him they would work through any complications that should arise. It wasn't as frightening now as it had been, but the future was still unknown, and she needed to square with that.

"I would like them to, yes." His grin was positively infectious, and she couldn't help but smile back. "Also, I asked my valet to take special care in dressing tonight, which meant I had to borrow this waistcoat from Duncan at the last minute."

"It's lovely." The rich sapphire silk embroidered with silver swirls drew her attention to his flat abdomen. "I do adore a man in evening attire." There was a matching sapphire stick pin in the starched folds of his exquisitely knotted cravat. What did it say about her that she wanted nothing more than to unwind that length of silk so she could kiss the skin she uncovered?

"Thank you. I'd hoped to look especially put together for you tonight." Excitement twinkled in his eyes as if he had a secret that he refused to tell.

"Why? I vastly prefer seeing you either in a state of undress or stripped down to your breeches like you do before getting into the boxing ring." It was useless to deny, even to him, that she found him handsome and far too attractive and tempting.

Those hazel pools darkened a bit, and his attention dropped briefly to her décolletage before he met her gaze. "That can easily be arranged before the night is over if you're of a mind."

Another wave of heat smacked into her. She fanned her face with a hand since she'd forgotten to bring her actual silken fan with the mother-of-pearl handles. "Enough, Lord Wexley, else we'll be for scandal right here near the wallflowers." With a furtive movement of her eyes, she indicated the young—and not so young—ladies sitting on the delicate chairs with gilt-painted legs who all wore the same expressions of longing as they watched the current set wind down.

"At least that would give them something of interest to watch," he said in a whisper, "or something to strive toward," he added with a wink. "It appears there will be a waltz next, so will you please partner me?"

"I will." How could she not? As she laid the fingertips of one hand on his sleeve and he led her to an open space on the dance floor, she smiled.

Obviously, she enjoyed the exercise dancing provided, but he was so handsome that a selfish part of her deep down wanted the female population at the ball to know he was hers. Additionally, she would have his undivided attention on the dance floor. Since that last coupling, something had shifted within her and she might like him more than was good for her, but that didn't negate that she was mildly annoyed with him due to feeling that he was holding something important back from her. Did not trust her with the information?

"I have long waited for a moment such as this," he admitted in a barely audible whisper as they stood in the proper position.

"Why? It is merely a waltz." Regardless of what her father had said that morning, she was still a bit frightened of having her wings clipped if she eventually consented to being with him for a lifetime.

"A waltz with the woman I admire above all others."

Then there was no time for further conversation or even his

charm, for the opening notes of the waltz broke upon the air, and he set them into motion, but flutters continued to bedevil her belly. Of course he was everything a gentleman should be, and between his grin that made her want to indulge in scandalous things as well as the tender touch of his hand as it brushed along hers during the steps of the waltz, she couldn't help but worry over the reason he'd chosen to hide whatever his secret was from her.

During the course of the dance, they were often obliged to switch partners, and each time that happened, she fretted that he was going to do something stupid… like asking her to marry him tonight. Was that the secret and the reason he was evasive?

Good heavens, I don't need this right now. I'm not ready!

By the time she partnered with him again for the last steps of the waltz, she'd worked herself into a tizzy.

He frowned. "Why do you look like you're ready to dump my body in the Thames?"

"That thought hadn't crossed my mind, but if you don't tell me what you are hiding, perhaps I shall." But she smiled sweetly at him as the dance came to an end and a spate of polite clapping followed.

"I suppose this is what I'm in store for for choosing a woman with spirit and a backbone, hmm?" But he winked as he led her to the nearest wall. "There is a very good reason why I am holding something back from you, and I don't wish for that knowledge to ruin our night."

She crossed her arms beneath her breasts and narrowed her eyes. "Tell me."

"Fine." A sigh escaped his throat. "I, uh…" He cleared his throat. "I have filled a last-minute opening at a bare-knuckle match that's set to take place just before dawn tomorrow morning."

"Why would you be fearful to tell me that? You' have always maintained that you'd enter more bouts, and I've told you I wouldn't stop you."

"This is true, but there is more."

"I see." Shock pummeled through her insides. "Why are you going?"

"One of the prize fighters dropped out due to a concussion he'd sustained at a tavern fight last night, so I was asked. Thanks to Duncan." Alexander shoved a hand through his hair, leaving it even more luxuriously flipped to one side. "My brother has quite the talent for advertising matches and getting us Stapleton boys placement."

"I have no doubts. One of these days, Lord Frampton will find his charm only goes so far." But none of that made her happy. "Who is your opponent? Is he more skilled than you?"

"I should probably keep that to myself if I wish to remain in one piece ahead of the bout."

"Ah, so you *do* have a secret. Who is it?"

"I don't want to say."

She tried to relax, but it didn't help, so she lowered her voice. "Damn you, Alex, tell me this instant. There have never been lies between us, and I don't intend to start now."

For long moments, while another country reel assembled on the parquet dance floor, Alexander stared at her. Finally, he nodded. "Colin MacIntosh."

"What?" She sucked in a breath, for it felt as if she'd been punched in the breadbasket and was winded. "Colin? My former fiancé, Colin?"

"Yes." His Adam's apple bobbed with a hard swallow. "Which is why I didn't want to tell you in the first place... Until I'd won, of course."

"How could you?" Fear played icy fingers up and down her spine.

"What? He's an opponent who is known to you. I'm not worried. I've fought all sorts and sizes of partners."

"But you haven't gone against Colin. And he's already threatened you!" When her voice began to rise, she quickly modulated it but couldn't calm herself. "He's going to kill you. In fact, he probably 'encouraged' that other boxer to drop out because he knew you or Duncan would fill in the gap."

"You don't know that." Hurt jumped into his eyes. "Besides, with the prize purse, I can make strides into renting a townhouse, which is the first step in sorting my life so that I'll look more attractive for a future. With you."

Dear heavens, he was adorable and dedicated to the cause and the hope that she would marry him, but she couldn't let that distract her. "You are more of a nodcock than I thought if you go through with this." If her tone sounded overly harsh, it was due to the fear and worry she held for him. Why couldn't he understand that she knew more about Colin than he did?

"Miss Tetford—Lydia—please listen to me," he implored in a whisper as he laid a hand on her shoulder. "Let me do this. If I win, I'll finally make my mark in the boxing world. Show that I can do this as well as my brothers."

While she understood that drive, he didn't take the danger seriously. "That is all well and good, but we both know you're *not* a strong boxer. That's not where your talents lie. We've had this discussion before."

He frowned and the hurt in his eyes deepened. "I'm not *that* rubbish."

"We shall discuss that later." Then she propped her hands on her hips. "Please don't do this." Tears choked the whispered plea. "Please."

"After everything, you don't believe in me." So much disappointment rang in his voice that it stabbed directly through her heart.

"No, that's wrong. I believe you can do anything you want… outside of a boxing ring!" When tears welled in her eyes, she made no move to stop them. "When you are inside that ring, I'm nearly worried sick—and I've only seen you fight publicly once!— and now that I know you'll fight Colin, I'm ready to cast up my accounts right here in this ballroom." Her heartbeat accelerated and she pressed her lips together. "I want so much to hide you away and protect you."

He snorted. "That is my duty to you."

"Perhaps, but it applies to the woman in a relationship too. Why can a woman not worry over the man in her life?" When he didn't answer, she huffed out her frustration. "None of this means I am not incredibly proud of you, Alexander, for I am." Despite them being in a crowded ballroom, she briefly laid a palm to his cheek. "Everything you're doing? Everything that will affect your future—our future—makes me trust you even more, but this worry that I have for you? It means I think you should be practical while you're chasing dreams."

"Did you ever err on the side of caution or concern when fighting the patriarchy in order to study medicine?"

Heat went into her cheeks. "We are not talking about me."

"Coward." But fondness softened the word. "Lydia, please." He took her hands in his. "I must do this to prove to Duncan and Lewis I'm not the weakest link in our business."

"They don't think that, and if they do, I'm happy to set them straight." For it was more than obvious to herself now. She loved him, quite desperately, and she would do anything to keep him safe and in one piece, but she also knew that if she didn't want her wings clipped in a marriage, she couldn't do the same to him.

That provoked a grin from him. "Well, then, I also need to prove to you that I *have* a future and am capable of being more than a bachelor with little to no responsibility." One of his brown eyebrows rose in challenge.

Would he always throw her words back in her face? A sigh escaped her. "Renting a townhouse is the first step."

"Yes, I know, which is why I need that prize purse."

"We shall get by… er, but that is in the future. You don't *need* to go through with this bout."

"If that is truly how you feel, I'll withdraw." His shoulders drooped, and in that moment, he appeared so glum that she lost another piece of her heart to him in that moment.

"No, don't." For long moments, she remained quiet. "I'm

sorry I said that early on after meeting you. Since then, you have certainly impressed me beyond what I ever expected."

Hope lit his eyes. "It's true, though, and has been the kick in the arse I needed to look seriously at my life."

"Oh, Alexander." Now that she could clearly see a future between them, it terrified her to think of being married, especially to a viscount, which would mean responsibilities that ran at cross purposes with her goals, pulled her away from being a physician, but... he was worth that and more. "Fine."

Confusion lay stamped on his face. "Fine what?"

"Go to the bout."

"Truly?" His whole countenance filled with joy, and he stood tall once more.

"Yes. Go fight in the bout, and if you get your clock cleaned, I'll make sure you're patched up." She nodded even as knots of worry pulled in her belly. "But I'll be damned if I let you go alone." Then she cursed, which had surprise and a bit of heat crowding into his eyes. "My father is the attending physician in this bout, but he never said you were one of the fighters, nor did he mention Colin."

"A father will always try to keep his daughter safe, Lydia, so will any man who loves you." Though he shot her a speaking glance, she refused to have *that* conversation right now. "I'm sorry we've all lied to you about this. Perhaps I'm not the man you'd hoped."

"Pish-posh. That's not well done of you, so don't fish for compliments, but I'm bringing my bag to the bout just in case. *And* afterward, I'm going to give you a dressing down you'll not soon forget since you *persist* in being a nodcock."

His grin widened. Respect danced in his eyes. "You're a real brick of a woman, do you know that?"

"Stop." She snorted. "You'd better stay in one piece because I'm not nearly done with you for many reasons." The feeling of falling returned, and the longer he peered at her with that hunger in his gaze, the more she wished she could distract him with carnal endeavors, but that wouldn't be fair to either of them. Daring much, she took his hand. "Come with me."

"Where and why? Are we going to get up to scandal?" He squeezed her fingers. "I really shouldn't use up my strength before a bout but…"

"Do shut up, Wexley." She gave him a tug toward the double doors that would open into the back gardens. "Scandal, yes, but not the kind you're thinking of. We'll do this out in the open space of the square."

"Do what? Couple where anyone can see?"

"Of course not. I'm not that daring." As soon as he was able following the bout, though, she intended to bed him, and thoroughly. "However, I do want to quickly teach you a few moves in jujitsu tonight so you can use them in the ring."

"What?"

She shrugged. "For whatever reason, we haven't had a chance to do that whenever we're in the salon. Something always comes up as a distraction."

"As if I'm the only one to blame for that."

Finally, she allowed a tight smile. "You aren't, and your brothers are far too often underfoot, but that is beside the point."

Once outside, Lydia wasted no time in marching him through the back garden with its riot of blooms and the soft buzzing of summertime insects. Then she led him through a gate and onward out into the square. Thankfully, there wasn't anyone about at this time of night. Perhaps they were gone from London or otherwise occupied. Avoiding the illumination of a handful of the gaslights set around the square, she drew him into the shadows.

"This is a good stretch of level ground. We'll start here." There was no better way to teach someone the basics of jujitsu than to jump right in. So saying, she gripped one of his arms with both hands, dropped her hips, bent at her knees, and then with a cry, she used her strength and the leverage of her hip to flip him over her body.

"What the hell?" The viscount stared up at her with shock etched on his face. "You could have at least warned me."

"Why? You won't warn an opponent in the ring, and neither will they give you that same courtesy. You'll soon find that these types of defenses rely heavily on using hips and leg strength, as well as the strength of one's body." When she offered him a hand to help him up, he took it, but then he yanked on her arm, pulling her down and quickly put his body atop hers.

"What's good for the goose is good for the gander, hmm?"

Oh, he had no idea, poor man. "And we've arrived at move number two—the armbar submission. I'm going to talk you through it as I demonstrate *on* you."

He was still grinning. "I rather doubt you can flip me."

It was another thing he'd prove wrong in. "Grab your partner's neck to break down their posture." She did so by slipping a hand about his nape. "Then you will step on their hip on the same side you're holding them and push your knee against their shoulder to keep them from pulling their arm out." As she spoke, she performed the move on him. "Next, push off on your opponent's hips to bring your body perpendicular to theirs." When she did so with only a bit of effort on her part, Lydia smiled. "Afterward, clamp down on their shoulders to keep them from slipping out of your hold." When she did exactly that, he panted and grunted with the effort of trying to break it. "You might choose here to kick them on the back of the neck, but don't. Instead, in one motion, bring your other leg over their head and curl it down to keep everything tight." It was deuced difficult to perform this move in skirts, but she managed it. "To finish, grab the wrist and bridge your hips. In this posture, you can easily choke them until they either pass out or grow too weak that they'll release you, letting you get away."

Alexander tapped her on the shoulder as he gasped for breath. When she released him, he gulped in air. "So I could see within the demonstration."

She untangled their bodies enough that she could kneel between his splayed legs that were bent at the knees. "In jujitsu, the end goal is to weaken your attacker as well as get away. It is a more effective fighting technique than pummeling the stuffing out of each other."

"I don't know about that."

"You will, and it is an excellent way to put down a larger opponent. I have used a couple of these moves on Colin myself, so if I can do it, so can you." She raised an eyebrow, daring him to contradict her. "Each time you wind them or cut off their ability to breathe, you weaken them. Keep that in mind, and I will teach you this last one."

"Oh, please no. You've already nearly killed me." He shook his head as his body went taut, signaling he would soon leave.

"For the love of everything holy, Alexander, pay attention. This could mean the difference of life or death in that damned ring." Ignoring the waver in her voice, she nodded. "Thank you for the attention. This is called the standing guard break. It's fairly easy."

He groaned. "For you. Apparently, you've studied for years."

"Yes, but not *for* years, though I do enjoy keeping current on the skills, especially in this day and age, so I practice with my brother once a month."

"Why do I have the feeling Ian will be all too happy to have me replace him in those exercises?"

She snickered. "It's the least you can do, but we'll discuss that later." After blowing out a breath, she met his gaze. "All right, in this one, we assume that both you and your opponent are on the ground. Let's suppose he's trying to flip you over in order to pin you."

"He wishes," Alexander boasted.

Lydia ignored him and his ego. "If that is the case, you need to keep him on his back. It will be critical at this point to secure his arms, so attach your grip in his armpits." As she spoke, she did so. "Then straighten your arms and lean forward so you can walk up and gain your feet, but don't let go of his arms." As she demonstrated, the sound of fabric ripping filled the air, and she feared she lost the hem of her gown, but that didn't matter. "Once you're back on your feet, place your knees directly under your opponent's hips."

"Damn it, Lydia, you're going to snap my spine!" It sounded more like a whine than a complaint.

Again, she ignored him. "Move backward as if you are sitting in a chair and arch your back so that you can keep good balance if your opponent tries to get away. Above everything, keep his arms and shoulders facing downward while you're using your strength to lift him up. For me, I'll try and balance you on my thighs and hips." She blew out a breath, because this is where the move was complicated. And he was a bit heavy in this almost dead weight posture. Sweat dripped down her spine and broke out on her brow.

"Stop. You'll hurt yourself."

"No." She shook her head. "You need to remember this, Alexander. It's important." Keeping her breathing regulated, she held him off the ground with his head and upper body slanted downward. "It is critical to keep your opponent's shoulders downward because this keeps this at a disadvantage. If his arms flail, just keep him off balance."

"Easier said than done, I think."

She grunted. "To finish, place your open hand directly under their kneecap and push down to encourage their legs to open and release you." When she did so, she easily stepped to the side. "That leaves him on the ground, where you can either punch him in an effort to help him stay there, or assume a different defensive posture if he scrambles to his feet."

Finally, the viscount stood up and faced her. "That was incredible. Thank you."

"Perhaps, but it might save your sorry arse if you can remember what I just taught you."

"As long as you are at that bout, I'll remember." Then he pulled her into his arms and kissed her soundly. "I'll hold my own against him, Lydia. I promise."

Tears welled in her eyes as she nodded. "I know you will, and if you don't, I'll beat him bloody with my bag, and society can go hang." Then she looped her arms about the breadth of his shoulders, rose onto her toes, and kissed him back.

Yes, they would get along splendidly as long as they allowed each other the space to spread their wings.

Chapter Sixteen

August 20, 1817
An hour before dawn
Somewhere between Borehamwood and Bushey
Hertfordshire, England

ALEXANDER TRIED TO take deep breaths to help circumvent his nerves. He'd ridden in a traveling coach to the place where the bout would take place. Accompanied by both of his brothers as well as the new countess, there hadn't been much talking on the relatively short journey; it seemed they were all lost in their own thoughts.

After he'd had that series of quick lessons by Lydia and the kisses they'd exchanged in the square, he had borrowed his brother's carriage and conveyed her home. But when he suggested that she come to the boxing ring with him and his brothers, she refused, saying that she would arrive with her father.

When he'd momentarily let panic take control, she shaken his shoulders and demanded that he look at her.

"If you think I'm going to abandon you in this, your hour of need, then you don't know me well at all." She'd held his hand between her hands while her gaze bore into his. "I will be there at that ring, encouraging you, supporting you, pointing out what you're doing wrong." Though she'd chuckled, it was a very watery affair. "Now, I'm going to change my clothing, but I promise to be there, exactly when you need me."

That talk had the power even now to pull a grin from him. *I need you now, Lydia.* When he opened his eyes, Lewis and his wife were staring at him. "What? Are you already thinking I'll fail out there?"

Oddly, it was Cecilia who answered. "No, of course not. I believe we are merely concerned about you, especially when discovering who your opponent is."

He nodded. "I shouldn't have agreed to enter the bout, but I have much to prove, to all of you." As he sent his gaze about the interior of the coach, saw the concern in his family's eyes in the illumination from the carriage lantern, he sighed. "Additionally, I would like to clean that man's clock for what he's done to Lydia, but regardless, I will give it my all."

Duncan jabbed him in the ribs, for they shared a bench. "I'll wager you won't make such a bad showing as Lewis when he had his shoulder dislocated."

"Ha!" Lewis shook his head. "I still managed to win that bout as well as the prize purse."

"You did, but you continue to have trouble with that shoulder," the countess gently reminded him. "You can prove so stubborn at times."

Alexander snorted. "We *all* can, but that doesn't need to be a detriment. Sometimes that is the only thing that keeps us motivated." He put a hand on the door latch. "Countess, no offense, but it would be in your best interests to stay in the coach. You are still dressed in your ballgown, and since you *are* a new countess, I'd hate for your reputation to be tossed in the gossip mill just to watch me fight."

She glanced at Lewis. "Do you wish for me to remain here?"

Clearly conflicted, his older brother bounced his gaze between her and Alexander. "He is correct. Will you be all right for about an hour? The driver will be around in the event you need something."

"Yes. I have a book with me. Send Duncan back to the carriage with periodic updates, or if he's the knee man, come yourself."

"I will," Lewis said while taking her hand and bringing it to his lips.

Her giggle filled the interior of the coach, but she slipped her regard to Alexander. "Best of luck tonight."

"Thank you." Then he pushed the door open, kicked down the steps, and finally exited the vehicle.

As Duncan removed the lantern from the outside of the coach, Lewis spoke in low tones to the driver, no doubt telling him to look after the countess. The dark shadows of a wooded area that framed the meadow where the boxing ring had been roped off stood like silent sentinels. At the horizon, the first faint illumination that would herald the dawn glimmered, but it would be at least a half hour before sunrise. That didn't matter, for there was a steady stream of not only carriage traffic leading toward the meadow but also foot traffic. Crowds were beginning to form, and from what Alexander had been told, his bout wouldn't be the only one that day, for the organizers had planned another after midnight.

Clearly, the sport was gaining popularity.

"Let's go," Lewis said as he came back into their group. "How are you feeling this morning, Alexander? You seem brimming with confidence."

He nodded. "I'm good. Anxious to start, frankly."

"Good. That's better than your usual glum attitude and will take you much further."

Duncan huffed. "Leave the poor man alone. He's prone to nerves already."

"Stop, the two of you," Alexander hissed as they approached the roped-off area. "I am trying to quiet my mind before the bout begins." He looked at Duncan. "Since the crowds are building, go see if you can find out the odds, or at the very least encourage them to throw their support behind me."

"Good idea. I'll be back before the bout starts." Then he loped off in the direction of the crowds.

Lewis walked beside him until they found out which corner theirs would be. "I know why you're doing this."

"Because boxing is in our blood?" Truly, he didn't wish to have a philosophical discussion right now.

"There is that, but you've fallen tip over tail for Miss Tetford and want to marry her." It wasn't a question. "I'm sensing that things have progressed in that quarter since last we talked about her."

Since it was useless to deny, Alexander nodded. "This is true. If I win the prize purse, I'll use it to put down a deposit on a modest townhouse to rent."

"A noble idea indeed."

Now was the opening he'd been hoping for. "One thing more. If I win tonight, will you let me be the manager of the salon instead of the bookkeeper?" When Lewis said nothing, Alexander rushed onward. "I believe I have a talent for management, and since I've been more or less doing that task along with the books in your absence, why not make it official?"

His brother frowned. "Who would take the accounting position? Surely not Duncan. He's the most careless person I've ever seen around coin."

"No, of course not. God, that would be a mistake." Alexander shook his head. "Why can your wife not do it? That is, until we can find someone else that we trust. Cecilia is amazing with a ledger book, if you've ever seen her work."

"As a matter of fact, I have, and you're not wrong." Lewis stroked his chin and finally nodded. "If you win, I'll formally give you the position of manager. After the first of the year, for unless I miss my guess, if you manage to win Miss Tetford's hand, she'll practically demand a wedding trip, and then there are the holidays. Best start everything with a clean slate after the old year passes."

"That makes sense." Pride welled in his chest. "Thank you. I won't let you down in this new endeavor." He might disappoint in the ring, but never in management. "Also, there is this." From the pocket of his waistcoat, he pulled out a silver filagree ring band with small square-shaped emeralds embedded in the metal. "It is nothing magnificent, but Mama let me remove it from one of her collections. At some point soon, I hope to propose to Lydia."

"Why did you bring it with you tonight?" Then Lewis' eyebrows rose. "You were going to ask her at the ball." Again, not a question.

"Yes, and when I saw her in that gown, I knew it was the right thing to do. And I especially knew it after she took me outside and gave me jujitsu lessons to help bring down my opponent tonight."

"I know exactly what you mean. There is something extraordinary when we realize everything we've ever wanted can be found in one incredible woman." Lewis grinned. "I'm truly happy for you." He went beneath the rope, and when Alexander followed, he nodded. "Then I hope you have all the fortune in the world this morning." Then he glanced up, and nodded once more. "It would seem there is someone else who wishes to have a word with you before the bout. I'll just go and introduce myself to the officials and greet Dr. Tetford."

As soon as the name reached his ears, Alexander tucked the ring into the waistcoat pocket and glanced around. When he saw Lydia, he gawked, for she was either the most emboldened woman he'd ever met or the most scandalous.

Perhaps both.

Dressed in the garb of a young stable hand—and where the devil had she acquired such an outfit?—not even the fiery hair scraped back from her skull and fixed in a tight bun beneath a cap could disguise the fact she was a woman. There was no mistaking the large, green eyes or the way her curves were on display despite the gray tweed jacket and dark breeches.

"Lord Wexley," she said in a low voice as she reached the rope.

He nodded. "Miss Tetford," he greeted in a whisper. As of yet, there was no one within earshot, so the risk of scandal was at a minimum. "I'm glad to see you." Knowing she was there pumped courage through his soul.

"I told you I would be." She pointed to the black bag at her booted feet. "And if you're pummeled into the ground, I'm here to pick up the pieces and patch you up." Then her chin trembled as she raked her gaze up and down his person. "Though I know why you're doing this and why I need to let you, I still worry for you."

Daring much, he briefly took her hand. "Not only will I survive, but I'll also thrive."

"I believe that, but I will say a prayer for you all the same." When the crowd became a bit frenzied, she turned her head to glance at the opposite corner. "Damn. Colin has arrived."

"Keep your attention on me." He would do well to do the same with her. "Just know that your being here has already helped tremendously. When he met her gaze, the emotions there nurtured the kernel of hope inside his chest. "I need to prepare for the bout, but will you stay close?"

"Of course. Papa is over there, but he'll pace around the ring as he did before. I'll keep my position in your corner, for there is no way I'm going near *him*." She indicated Colin with her chin.

"Good. You can serve as my water boy if you'd like, else you'll not be able to remain in the ring." He nodded, for having her close would help keep his thoughts focused. "My brothers are nearly here."

"I'll do it, because I'm not leaving you to your own devices. We saw how that ended the last time." But she tempered the words with a tremulous smile. "Be strong, be fast on your feet, and remember what I taught you last night at the ball."

"I will."

"And take this." She dug into a pocket, then withdrew a lady's handkerchief. "I put a bit of my perfume on it. The lavender will soothe your anxiety."

"Thank you." There was no time, nor the privacy needed to kiss her, so that affection would have to wait. As his brothers came under the rope, Alexander began the task of undressing. Once more, his nerves felt as if they were crawling through his body, but he lifted the handkerchief to his nose and inhaled Lydia's familiar scent. Just as she'd said, a bit of calm came over him. He gave it to her. "Keep this clean for me. I'll need it later."

Then Duncan stared hard at her. "Miss Tetford?"

"Yes." She nodded with a tight smile. "I'm not leaving him alone or with the two of you. He needs someone with far more logic and a different perspective."

Both of his brothers chuckled, but it was Lewis who responded. "Glad to have you aboard, Miss Tetford. It seems you'll fit in just fine with the Stapleton connection."

Into Lewis' ear, Alexander hissed, "Don't rush my fences. I still need to survive the bout."

"You will. There is no doubt in my mind you'll show both me and Miss Tetford for fools." And he grinned. "Finish undressing. They're almost ready to start."

Chapter Seventeen

N O SOONER HAD he handed his clothing to Lewis, for the earl would serve as his corner man during the bout, which meant he wasn't allowed inside the ring once the fight started, than the crowd roared as the first rays of the sunrise broke the horizon. Duncan would be his knee man, with Lydia acting as water boy. Though it was the high summer, being stripped down to only his breeches left him vulnerable to the bit of a chill in the dawn air.

His gaze fell on Lydia, who knelt in the corner. "I will make you proud."

She snorted. "I am already proud of you, nodcock," she said softly. "Clean his clock; he is not a nice man."

Then Lewis clapped a hand on his shoulder. "Focus and re-member what Papa taught us. Footwork will win the day."

Finally, Duncan perched on a convenient large rock sitting in the corner. "Hell with that. Make it ugly. Bring the beast down any way you can."

That prompted a grin from Alexander. "Thank you, every-one. I'll do my best." How much did he love his family?

Then a shrill whistle blast pierced the air. It was time.

With a little shove from Lewis, Alexander approached the center of the boxing ring. He narrowed his eyes on the large, beefy man who was his opponent—Colin MacIntosh. Damn, he was built like a rock and had about six inches on his own five-foot nine-inch height. The size of his hands were like small hams. Black hair that had a tendency to curl covered his head, not done in any sort of style, and a thick mat of matching hair decorated the upper portion of his barrel chest. Pure dislike glittered in his beady eyes beneath shaggy eyebrows, and there was no doubt in Alexander's mind this man wished to pound him into the dirt.

"Once I break you, Wexley, I'm going to reclaim Miss Tetford," his opponent growled as he slammed a fist into the palm of his other hand.

"I'll wager you would need to kill me first." Under no circumstances would Alexander allow this man anywhere near Lydia.

Not again.

"Gentlemen, keep it civil until we start." A tall, bespectacled man stood in the middle of the boxing square and held up a hand. No doubt he would act as a caller this morning, and he might also have invested funds into the bout. It was difficult to tell. "We're about to begin." When the noise from the crowd died down somewhat, he continued, "Today's match is between one of the darlings of the bare-knuckle world, the Honorable Mr. Alexander Stapleton, or you may know him as the Viscount of Wexley." A roar erupted from the men assembled as spectators. "And his rival, the man who's beaten countless boxers in the Lake District as well as in Scotland, Mr. Colin MacIntosh." Another cheer rose from the crowd. Clearly, the man had supporters.

It didn't matter that the onlookers' loyalties were split. Alexander didn't care about any of that. He would do what he was capable of and make the people closest to him proud. When he risked a glance back at his corner, his gaze met Lydia's. She stared back with rounded eyes and her lips set in a hard line, but she gave him a nod of encouragement.

It was enough, and damn but he wanted to clean Colin's clock.

By this time, another man had entered the ring to stand next to the tall fellow. He held up a hand for silence.

"I am Mr. Applegate, your judge for the bout this morning." The man was someone easily forgettable with absolutely no discernable features that would be remembered. Even his brown hair beneath the top hat was mousy and plain. "We will, of course, keep the bout going until one of these men manages to pin his opponent for ten seconds, or one of them manages to knock the other out cold."

A roar from the crowd followed. Spectators of bare-knuckle fighting were a bloodthirsty lot.

Then Dr. Tetford joined the other two men. "Good morning. I'm the physician here, so if you do suffer any sort of injury, I'll help you through it." When his gaze met Alexander's, one of his eyebrows slightly lifted. "May the best man win."

Just as surreptitiously, Alexander nodded.

From his position in front, Colin uttered a growl and shifted his weight from foot to foot. "This fight will go quickly, Wexley." He flashed a grin of premature victory. "I can't imagine an ineffective boxer like ye will last past perhaps two rounds." The Scottish brogue was more than a bit prominent in his voice.

Hot annoyance surged through his chest. "Bragging a little too early, are you, MacIntosh?" For lack of something to do and to hide his nerves, he fisted his hands, then relaxed them a few times in succession to crack the knuckles. Afterward, he lifted his arms above his head and stretched out the muscles in his torso, for he had a feeling it would be better to feel loose during the first round. "No man is invincible. Even you," he couldn't help but add.

The bigger man snorted. "I'll wager my record is better than yers."

"That means absolutely nothing." Again, he glanced over to his corner where Lydia was quietly talking with Duncan. In the dim illumination of a not yet full dawn, she appeared as a slight young man, but he would do anything to touch her cheek, share a brief kiss for luck and strength, merely to know she believed in him. When she looked over her shoulder at him and smiled, confidence surged through his veins. When the other three men left the boxing ring, Alexander assumed his first position, fists at the ready, body taut and balanced. "May the best man win, MacIntosh, in body and spirit."

Because, after all, no matter who was declared the victor at the end of the bout, he would still be proud of himself.

He hoped.

A whistle blast split the air. The judge shouted, "Remember, rounds will continue until one man is put on the ground and unable to stand after three seconds. Go!"

The crowd roared in anticipation.

Alexander and his opponent circled each other, prowled through the meadow grass of the eight-foot roped-off area. The doctor as well as the host walked the outside edges of the ring. How the devil should he bring this beast down? Knowing how difficult it was the last time he'd come to blows with Colin in Hyde Park, he might need to change his tactics and fall to what Lydia had taught him last night. Excitement buzzed at the base of his spine, prompting him into movement. *I need that prize purse.* And the one person standing in his way of that goal was his opponent.

Hoping for the element of surprise, he threw the first punch. It connected solidly with Colin's cheek, but the bigger man didn't seem to notice.

The other man grinned as he struck out a powerful fist that barely clipped Alexander's shoulder. "Is that the best ye've got, Wexley? I expected more from a son of the great George Stapleton."

He danced away, much to the crowd's roar of approval. "I've barely started." He swung a fist, but the bigger man easily dodged the punch.

"This round belongs to me." MacIntosh struck with a fast uppercut to his chin that jarred his teeth together. He followed it with a jab to Alexander's middle.

Pain exploded through his face and stomach, but he held his ground and returned the volley, tagging the bigger man in the chin and abdomen. After that, they were into the thick of the first round as blows rained and fists pummeled, landing on solid flesh in rhythmic intervals. The thud of fists hitting skin echoed in his ears. One of his right hooks had MacIntosh staggering backward, but at the last second, the man didn't fall. Neither did Lewis when retaliation occurred.

Much to the roar of the crowd. For or against, it didn't much matter who they wanted to win, for Alexander largely ignored them.

Minutes ticked by that seemed like hours. Blood trickled along the side of his face from a wound that had opened at his left eyebrow from one of his opponent's blows. His breath grew labored, but he defended well enough before the round was finally called.

Grateful for the brief reprieve, Alexander trudged to his corner, as did MacIntosh.

Winded, he sat heavily on Duncan's offered knee. "I might have underestimated MacIntosh's stamina." He met Lydia's gaze as skies lightened as the sun continued to rise. "What are his weak points?"

"Being illiterate?" She shrugged while Lewis snorted with derision from outside the ring. "Truthfully, though, he is a powerhouse, but he does favor his right ankle. I remember him saying that he'd broken it once in his youth." She handed him a ladle full of cool water from an oaken bucket. "Just stay alert."

"Right." He nodded. "I'll bear that in mind."

"Stop complaining." Duncan gave his shoulder a little shake. "You are unconsciously letting his size faze you. Keep your strikes fast and low, then use your power for punches to the head."

"I will." Alexander wiped sweat from his brow with a rag. "Thank you." After taking a deep sip of the cool water from the ladle, he handed it back to Lydia.

"You've faced similar men before." Lewis kneaded the muscles in Alex's shoulders. "If you must, try to wear him down, or if you want to play dirty, use your heel in his weak ankle."

"I trust my skill, but if worse comes to worst, I'll try different tactics he might not expect." And he could thank Lydia for that.

Another whistle blast announced the start of round two, and with a groan, Alexander stood. He returned to the middle of the ring to face off with his opponent once more.

"Give up, Wexley," MacIntosh growled. "Accept ye aren't as good as yer brothers."

"You don't think I already know that?" It was always a worry, but he didn't take the statement personally. "But I'd rather die," he tossed back.

"I can arrange that. Two well-timed punches will bash in yer skull."

"You won't have the chance." Movement at one side of the ring caught his eye. Damn it! Lydia in her groomsman clothing had changed position apparently for a better view, concern etched on her face.

Do this for her, he reminded himself.

Unfortunately, in that small moment of distraction, a hard uppercut to his jaw had him staggering back several steps. The crowd roared and as one entity they surged forward. Pain exploded through his face and jawline, but he kept his feet and hoped his teeth weren't broken from being smacked together. With a roar, Alexander lunged toward MacIntosh. He landed quick jabs to the bigger man's stomach, cheek and chin.

The Scot reeled and retreated before gathering himself and charging at Alexander to exchange blows in close combat style.

Again and again, he drilled his fists into the bigger man's body, and in some places on the hard form, his blows felt as if they glanced off his skin, and the boxer wouldn't fall. There was simply no extra fat on the man.

What the hell do I do now?

MacIntosh got off a few good punches of his own, and the stubbornness that Alexander had always been known for kept him on his feet, though winded and aching. "Give up, Wexley. I tire of fighting inferior partners."

"Too bad, because I'm only getting started," he said in response, even though he wanted to curse from the pain in his head and abdomen.

Amusement lit the other man's eyes. "Ye are an embarrassment to the sport."

"Perhaps, yet I'm still standing." And he delivered a swift right hook to the other man's cheek that sent the other man spinning about. As the crowd cheered, MacIntosh stumbled but he didn't fall.

Then the round was once again called without a clear victor. *Thank God.*

Alexander stumbled back to his corner, dropping heavily onto Duncan's bent knee, panting and trying his best not to cast up his accounts. Every point on his body hurt and throbbed with pain. "The man won't go down. It's like beating a brick wall."

"You are going to need to do much better else he'll drill you into the ground as your strength flags," Duncan hissed, as Lydia plied him with water. "It doesn't seem like you want this victory much."

"That's a lie." Frankly, he was at a loss as to how to proceed.

"Then make quick work of him."

"I'm trying, but he's like a mountain." He stood, glancing at Lydia and handing her back the ladle. "What the hell should I do?"

"Alexander, concentrate." When their gazes connected, she offered a tremulous smile but worry clouded her green eyes. "He will kill you if given half the chance. Incorporate jujitsu moves on him that keep him on the ground. If you have a chance, use the strength of your body, use your forearms around his neck to choke him, make him woozy, then put him down with a swift punch to the temple. That's going to be your only chance."

"Right." That might be the best option at this point. While Duncan wrapped his busted knuckles with thin strips of cotton—

Lewis wasn't present so he must have gone off to give his wife an update—he shared a look with Lydia. Heated sensation went through him, followed by a blossom of hope that lifted his flagging spirits. They had a future together, he could feel it, and damn it all, he would ask for her hand at some point today. He wanted her more than he wanted to win that prize purse.

"Get your head out of your arse and focus on besting that man," Duncan demanded as he finished wrapping Alexander's knuckles and palms. "You have to get back out there. Remember, Papa taught all of us to fight, and he never believed you were the worst of us. You just have a different skill set." He gave him a push, which refocused his thoughts.

"Thank you for that." Shoving a hand through his sweat dampened hair, Alexander made his way back to the middle of the ring while the crowd roared its approval.

The judge blew his whistle again. The next round was about to begin.

There was no time to ponder his next course of action, for MacIntosh barely waited for the whistle sound to fade before he took a swing at Alexander, catching him on the shoulder so hard that he spun about.

"Shit." Pain ebbed down Alexander's arm, but he couldn't think about that right now. All too soon, he was caught up in a whirlwind of blows that left him reeling and very much on the defensive. When one of the bigger man's fists drilled into his gut, pain swamped him, had him doubled up with it. He returned the volley and was fortunate enough that his fist found purchase on MacIntosh's nose. The sickening crunch of cartilage was satisfying, as was the burst of blood down the bigger man's face.

Scrapping ensued, and since there were no longer gentleman-ly rules here, he welcomed the breakdown of decorum, for that meant he could fight the way Lydia had shown him.

Alexander breathed deeply in an effort to find calm and to ignore the agony his body was in. He executed a quick double uppercut, one with each fist to MacIntosh's gut and chin, and in the precious seconds that followed, when the Scot teetered, he slammed a heel into the other man's right ankle.

With a cry of anguish, MacIntosh finally hit the ground, and the crowd roared from either approval or denial.

"Damn you, Alex, this is your moment! Use it!" The cry of encouragement from Lydia was somehow heard over the crowd's noise and the thunder of his pulse in his own head.

Before he could deliver another blow, the Scot reached out, clamped a beefy hand around his calf and then yanked. Alexander lost his balance, tumbling to the sweet meadow grass, and seconds later, the bigger man was on top of his body in an attempt to pin his shoulders.

"Concede the match, Wexley." MacIntosh might have strength on his side and the current upper hand, but he hadn't won yet. "Ye're nearly gone."

"Not yet." Though his endurance wavered, he refused to give up, for he wanted Lydia proud of him, wanted also to show his brothers that he wasn't useless in the boxing world.

Briefly, he closed his eyes as he fought with the other man to keep his shoulders from the ground. What had Lydia said about the two moves she'd shown him—the armbar submission?

Then he put that into action and hoped to God that he re-membered. He ignored the yells from the crowd, ignored his brother's calls, ignored everything to concentrate on Lydia's dulcet instructions in his mind. Reaching up, he grabbed MacIntosh's neck. At the same time, he placed his right foot on the big man's hip on that same side. Before MacIntosh could do anything else, he pushed his knee against the man's shoulder to prevent him from pulling his arm out of the hold."

"What the hell, Wexley? This isn't boxing," MacIntosh said as confusion shadowed his face.

"Ha!" He blew out a breath of pain as sweat rolled down his back and face. "We left boxing the moment you played dirty."

Then, with a groan, he pushed off on the big man's hips. It took a couple of tries, but he finally was able to bring his body perpendicular to the other boxer's.

"Let me up!" MacIntosh's growled demand had no effect on Alexander.

"No." Lydia's words and her instructions were so clear in his mind. With a bit more confidence and ease, he clamped down on Colin's shoulders to keep them from slipping out of his hold. He panted, but the move was fairly easy, even when MacIntosh thrashed about in an effort to break it. As he held onto the bigger man, his heel dug into the back of the Scot's neck, and with a surge of his strength, he brought his other leg over Colin's head. Though his muscles screamed in protest, Alexander curled his leg down and effectively pinned the other man to the ground.

The crowd roared.

Emboldened and knowing MacIntosh was well and truly immobilized, Alexander grabbed the bigger man's wrist, and with his hips, he continued to keep him pinned. As his forearm landed against Colin's throat, he locked onto his own wrist and squeezed. "It's time we end this bout, don't you think?" he managed to say around clenched teeth.

"Get… off… me," the other man gasped out.

"Not a chance." And he continued to hold onto the Scot as his opponent's face turned red.

"Cheating."

"Perhaps, but this is to my advantage, and no one has cried foul yet." Exerting a bit more force, he tightened every muscle in his body. As his stamina waned, MacIntosh's thrashing quieted. His gasps became thinner, and his eyelids fluttered.

"Go to sleep, MacIntosh." When the other man went still in his hold, Alexander didn't waste any time. Though blood dripped down his face and onto his chest to mingle with sweat, he quickly scrambled to his feet. He couldn't remember how many wounds he'd sustained. Pain screamed through his body, and he sucked in deep breaths. But when the Scot stirred and tried to scramble to his feet, Alexander knew this was his final chance. "I'm not retired just yet, you great oaf, and if you ever come near Miss Tetford again, I swear I will kill you." As wild yells came from the crowd, Alexander delivered a powerful punch to the side of Colin's face, where his jaw joined his temple.

For the space of a few painful heartbeats, the other man waited on his knees. Confusion, then realization, clouded his eyes, and finally, seconds later, his eyes rolled back into his head, and he fell to the grass, face first. Best of all, he didn't move again.

The crowd roared. His brothers whooped with victory. And Alexander bent at the waist with his hands at his knees. He cast up his accounts moments later.

The judge came over to make certain MacIntosh was down. When Dr. Tetford agreed, the judge counted down from ten. Then, "The winner of this bout is the Honorable Mr. Alexander Stapleton! Viscount Wexley has won the prize purse as well as bragging rights!"

Dear God, I've won.

Nearly a half hour later, he'd finished with all the well-wishers, and as the crowds thinned, he stumbled over to his corner. His thoughts weren't on the victory, but on Lydia. He frowned. "Where is Miss Tetford?" Damn, but his whole body hurt, and all he wanted to do was seek out his bed and lay in one spot for the next few days.

Lewis shrugged. "She left when you went down. Said she couldn't bear watching two ridiculous men in a ridiculous fight, and that she was going to her father's carriage to compose herself and get away from the crowds."

Odd. She promised to stay with me until the end.

"Did she go over to talk with MacIntosh?" He reached for his shirt, and damn if it wasn't the most painful thing to don that garment.

"As far as I know, she did not. She spoke briefly with her father, then took her bag and left." Happiness and pride mixed in his older brother's eyes. "Congratulations, though. That was magnificent."

"Thank you." In some agony, he shoved a foot into one of his boots. "Where's Duncan?"

"Where else? Working the crowd as well as titled men he might hook as investors in the salon." He glanced across the ring. "Dr. Tetford is trying to get my attention. Will you be all right here by yourself?"

"Yes." A groan left his throat as he tugged on the second boot. "I'm going after Lydia, for I wish to speak with her, quite urgently."

Lewis snorted. "You need the doctor."

"*She's* a doctor." Once he took up his waistcoat, he removed the ring from its pocket. "Bring home the remainder of my clothes, hmm?"

"Aren't you returning to London?"

"Yes, but I can't guarantee when." With another groan, he ducked under the rope.

"But what about claiming the prize purse?"

He waved a hand. "Go in my stead. This is more important." Then he narrowed his eyes. "And don't think to steal the coin. That is going toward a townhouse and my future."

While Lewis made a crude gesture, Alexander strode off in the direction of where all the vehicles had been parked. A few men in the crowd going that way congratulated him, and he acknowledged them with friendly nods or a grin. Eventually, as he winded his way through a veritable sea of black coaches and carriages, he spied Lydia with her back against one of them. Her eyes were closed, and as he drew closer, it was apparent she'd been crying. Moisture and silvery tracks of tears stained her face.

"Lydia."

She startled at the sound of his voice. Her eyes flew open. "Alexander!" When he thought she might throw herself into his arms, she took hold of his shirt instead and then shoved his back against the carriage. "I was beside myself with fear and worry! You could have been killed."

"But I wasn't." Though he wanted to grin, he didn't want her to think he made jest of her. "In fact, I won the bout, sweeting. I won!"

"What?" Shock shadowed her eyes as they rounded.

"I won." He nodded. "Once I got Colin down on the ground, he pounced, just as I knew he would, but then I employed some jujitsu on him, choked him with my forearm until he'd almost passed out, and finished him with a punch." As he grinned, pain went through his face once more. "I couldn't have done it without you."

Yet she'd left before the bout had ended.

"Oh." She lifted a hand, danced her fingertip along the side of his face, frowning when he winced. "I'm sorry I wasn't there. I couldn't bear to see you being hit any longer." Then she put her hand on her chest. "It hurt my soul."

"I can appreciate that." When he tried to move away from the carriage, she was quick to pin him against the side once more. "Lydia?"

The emotions in her eyes and reflected on her face made him catch his breath. "Is that all you would say to me? After everything?"

Confusion temporarily took hold of his brain, then he shook his head. "No, it's not. In fact, I left the ring amidst all the celebration, even before I was given the prize purse, so that I could come and check on you."

She bit her bottom lip, and that had the capacity to drive him wild. "You did?"

"Yes." He nodded.

"You look a fright."

"That is to be expected, and I feel like the very devil has had his way with me, but what I need to say to you is more important, for you are all I can think about." Knowing he couldn't move forward with his life until he'd secured her promise, he offered his palm and smoothed out his fist, revealing the silver filigreed ring on his palm. "I do not have the necessary brain capacity or the stamina to come up with a bunch of poetic words or an elaborate speech."

"Alex?" She bounced her gaze from his palm to his face.

"Quite frankly, I doubt you would appreciate any of that nonsense anyway, for you are the most stubborn, maddening, determined, truthful and boldest woman I have ever met." When she remained silent, he sighed. Even that hurt. "Marry me. I'm tip over tail for you, sweeting. Yes, in a mere two weeks, I'm in love with you. Sometimes a man just knows."

"Oh." Tears welled in her eyes. The drops fell to her cheeks, and she sniffled. "Yes."

"What?" In all honesty, he assumed he'd have to fight much harder to convince her. "Is that all *you* would say to *me?*"

She chuckled and cried all the harder. "What is there to say, Wexley? Like you, I have unexpectedly fallen in love with you, even when I fought this inevitability every step of the way." Shaking her head, she took the ring from his palm and held it up, caught between her forefinger and thumb. "I was terrified for you at the start of this bout, afraid you would be either maimed or killed, and I couldn't bear it because I only just realized I love you, couldn't imagine not having you in my life."

Dear God. He drew in a shuddering breath and let it out. "Does this mean…?"

"Yes." Lydia nodded. She took the ring and slipped it onto the fourth finger of her left hand. "I will marry you, and not only to keep you from making horrible decisions, but because you are the part of my soul I've been missing all these years." When he would have embraced her, she put a palm to his chest and held him steady. "But this doesn't mean I'm giving up my dreams. I still intend to work as an uncertified physician in my father's clinic, and I will not become the woman that society thinks I should be merely because we'll marry."

"I want you just the way you are, Lydia. The woman who stole my heart, or rather, bossed it out of me." He grinned, and his busted bottom lip protested the movement. "If you decide to lead me around by my nose for the rest of my life, you'll find no protests." He shrugged. "Who you are is refreshing; we complement each other, and I don't know of any other woman who could encourage or support or push me to be a better man than you."

"And I don't know of a man more in need of guidance than you." She continued to laugh through her tears as he feigned outrage. "Whatever man you want to be, I'll stand behind you and dare anyone to tell you nay. As long as we are together, there is nothing we can't tackle."

"I agree." He took her hand with its new adornment. "Is all well, then?"

"Yes, and I would advise you to kiss me now to make it official," she said in a choked whisper. "To convince that you are true, but then I'm going to give you a full examination, because I don't trust that you haven't truly broken yourself."

"Ah, sweeting, life is going to be quite interesting, I think." Then, with a gentle tug, he reeled her into his arms and tenderly kissed her. Even that brought him pain, but he didn't care. Finally, he'd won her, and she would soon be his wife. With a groan, he pulled away. "I'm in a considerable amount of pain just now, but that in no way reflects how I feel about you."

"Don't be an arse, Alexander." After she opened the door to the carriage, she assisted him inside the vehicle. "There will be other times to show me how you feel. In this moment, I'll clean you up and you can recline on one of the benches, for I asked my father to ride back to London with your brothers." As he settled on one of the well-squabbed benches, she instructed the driver to return to Town and her father's house. Once she joined him, she shook her head and tsked her tongue. "So much blood. It's a wonder you survived."

"Agreed, but I did, against the odds."

"Well, you *are* a Stapleton."

"Perhaps, but I rather think it is thanks to you." Perhaps that was all a man needed—the support and love of a good woman who believed in him no matter what. "In the end, it wasn't a boxing opponent who knocked me on my arse. As soon as you came into my life, I went down swinging... for love."

With a sigh while the pain sank into his battered body, he closed his eyes as she rummaged in her bag and the carriage lurched into motion.

No longer did he have no path, and he looked forward to every step he would tread upon it.

Epilogue

September 30, 1819
No 6 St. George Street
Hanover Square, Mayfair
Westminster, England

Amp; LEXANDER CAME INTO the drawing room of the townhouse he shared with his wife, and he grinned to see her sitting on a low sofa with a cheerful fire dancing behind an ornate metal frame. Well, Lydia was napping if truth be told, while their sixteen-month-old son Andrew quietly fussed from his position tucked against her side with her arms about him. With a mop of red-brown curls and hazel eyes, the boy resembled them both.

"What's wrong, little man?" he said in a soft voice as he scooped the boy up and cuddled him against his shoulder. "Mama not paying attention to you?" He chuckled as he carried the baby to a sofa across a table from where Lydia slept. After sitting down, he bounced the baby on his knee, made silly faces at him until his tears dried and giggles replaced them. "That's my sunny boy. No time for fussing, huh?"

From what they'd figured, the child had been a result of one of their couplings during that turbulent August when they'd first met. After Alexander had won the bout against Lydia's former fiancé, he had been true to his word and used the coin he'd earned as a down payment on a modest townhouse. They'd chosen Hanover Square for its location. It was close to the Stapleton Boxing Salon on Brook Street as well as the Tetford Clinic located in a nearby cul-de-sac just off Brook Street as well.

On the days when Lydia's father didn't work in the clinic, she filled in, and when she wasn't spending long hours there, she'd embraced her role as Viscountess Wexley with the same strength and determination that she did everything else in her life. Once little Andrew George had come along, she dropped down to two days a week at the clinic with the caveat that she would return to five days once the boy was more self-sufficient.

To compensate for her loss and since the clinic was quite popular with the general public, as well as healing the aches and pains rendered in the boxing salon, her father had hired another male doctor, a young man with ideals of his own. Fortunately for him, he didn't ruffle Lydia's rather forward-thinking mindset, so all was well there.

As for Alexander himself, he had been the official manager of the boxing salon since January of 1818, just as his brother Lewis had promised. Under his leadership, the salon had nearly doubled its membership as well as its private client roster. That meant Lewis was now exclusively taking care of the private clients, whether those lessons happened at the salon or at a private residence, and he was even in the process of creating a small salon of his own out of his home for the same purposes, as well as keeping his countess happy so she could practice sparring without needing to come into the salon.

In addition to running the salon, Alexander had taken on a few speaking engagements to various groups and clubs that taught people the basics of self-defense and how to stay vigilant in their own environments. During some of those talks, he would demonstrate the basics of jujitsu, for he and Lydia had continued to study that form of combat with a man from Japan after their marriage.

As for Duncan. Well, his younger brother had had quite the time of it before he'd finally found his own wife, but then, perhaps it had been the best to fit with his personality. His story was certainly an entertaining one, and sometimes he told the tale when they were all out in the club enjoying some time away from the family.

It was odd how the Stapleton brothers' lives had all changed in one fell swoop of a year.

When a flailing baby fist smacked Alexander in the nose, he was wrenched quickly from his wandering thoughts. "Don't like it when Papa woolgathers?"

The boy giggled and grinned, showing a few teeth that had come in.

Lydia awoke at that moment with a start and a gasp. She glanced about in disorientation, and when her gaze fell on him with the baby, she sighed in relief. "Good heavens, I thought he'd fallen out of my arms."

"Not a chance. You had him well contained." Alexander smiled at her, and once more he thanked whatever deity was listening for putting her into his life. "When I came in, you were dead to the world. No doubt everything on your schedule has exhausted you."

"Perhaps, but I do need to speak with you about that." With a yawn, she put herself into a more upright position but still lounged against the high back of that piece of furniture. The emotions in her eyes were difficult to read.

Knots of worry tugged in his gut. "Are you ill?"

"No." She shook her head, but then exquisite happiness lit her eyes. "When I was last in the clinic, I asked our midwife to come examine me." Another yawn interrupted her. "Where I thought I'd caught a summer head cold turned out to be another pregnancy."

"What?" He must have appeared frightening to his son, for the boy gave him a pout coupled with tear-filled eyes. Quickly putting on a happy face, he bounced Andrew on his knee again. "Did you hear what Mama said?" With a glance to her, he asked,

"Is it true?"

"Yes." She gave him a happy nod. "That is the reason I'm so exhausted and why I've been a watering pot of late." Then she met his gaze. "We'll have a new addition to our family in March. Are you happy, Alexander? You won't mind another baby?"

"Do I mind?" He peered at his son, then put tiny kisses all over the chubby cheeks, his chin, his forehead, and his belly through the gown until the boy giggled all over again. "I'm gloriously thrilled, sweeting. To have another child as a result of our love for each other?" Scooping Andrew up into his arms, Alexander stood, then relocated to Lydia's sofa. As soon as he sat beside her, the boy reached out his arms to his mama.

"I'm so glad." Once she'd settled their son in her lap, she found Alexander's gaze. "After we are certain this second child will thrive, I would like to take measures to stem any more pregnancies for a time. It will take all my energy and strength to look after two, as well as return to doctoring." Pleading mixed with hope in her eyes. "Are you of a same mind?"

"Of course." Did she not know by now he'd do anything for her? "I'd rather have you and the children in good health than keep you increasing for the next ten years." He leaned over and brushed his lips against hers. "Besides, I'll still have you, and that is all I have ever wanted since meeting you."

A faint blush filled her cheeks. "Rogue." But she smiled, and then the baby did too. "Ah, Alex, we are so fortunate, and I couldn't be any happier."

"I know exactly what you mean." He slipped an arm about her waist and pulled both her and the baby close. "And I am still in love with you."

"As I am with you." She laid her head on his shoulder. "Even if you are more of an arse than you should be," she added with a note of teasing in her voice.

"Managing baggage," he rebutted in a whisper but with a grin.

Life had a way of surprising a man, but the key to surviving all the turmoil was simply not to try and control it. Like the wind, sometimes a good push in a different direction led a man to places he'd never thought to go on his own.

The End

About the Author

Sandra Sookoo is a *USA Today* bestselling author who firmly believes every person deserves acceptance and a happy ending. Most days you can find her creating scandal and mischief in the Regency-era, serendipity and happenstance in Victorian America or snarky, sweet humor in the contemporary world. Most recently she's moved into infusing her books with mystery and intrigue. Reading is a lot like eating fine chocolates—you can't just have one. Good thing books don't have calories!

When she's not wearing out computer keyboards, Sandra spends time with her real-life Prince Charming in central Indiana where she's been known to goof off and make moments count because the key to life is laughter. A Disney fan since the age of ten, when her soul gets bogged down and her imagination flags, a trip to Walt Disney World is in order. Nothing fuels her dreams more than the land of eternal happy endings, hope and love stories.

Stay in Touch

Sign up for Sandra's bi-monthly newsletter and you'll be given exclusive excerpts, cover reveals before the general public as well as opportunities to enter contests you won't find anywhere else.

Just send an email to sandrasookoo@yahoo.com with SUBSCRIBE in the subject line.

Or follow / friend her on social media:
Facebook: facebook.com / sandra.sookoo
Facebook Author Page: facebook.com / sandrasookooauthor
Pinterest: pinterest.com / sandrasookoo
Instagram: instagram.com / sandrasookoo
BookBub Page: bookbub.com / authors / sandra-sookoo